SKYLA GRAY

The Imaginary Friend's Obsession

Monster Research Facility #3

Contents

Chapter One

I'm halfway through the workday, listening to a customer scream obscenities, when a bird slams into the window beside my desk. I jump in my seat, nearly dropping the phone.

"Are you even listening to me?" the customer shouts.

I swallow, pressing my hand to my pounding heart. "Of course I am, sir."

He resumes ranting about our TV plan's increased price, as if that's something I should be held personally accountable for. I stare at the smudged window and imagine the bird's broken body on the sidewalk three stories below. I only caught a glimpse of black and white feathers, but I think it was a magpie. How's that old rhyme go? *One for sorrow...*

It feels like a bad omen. And the others in the office are looking over at me. Whispering.

Noticing me.

I shrink down in my chair. It's not me they're staring at, I tell myself. It's just the window. I've been doing so well this time, making myself bland and forgettable. I've been succeeding for nearly a year without incident.

Nothing has happened that will shatter that façade of normalcy. Yet there's a strange prickling along the back of my neck, like someone is watching me. My stomach churns with dread. That bird…that bird bothers me.

The customer runs out of breath, and I take my chance to start talking about special loyalty discounts for valued customers. Still, feathers and blood linger in my mind.

I pull my coat tighter around myself. I'm always wearing it with winter approaching, even indoors with the heat on. Rainy Seattle is too far from the desert heat my body is accustomed to, and the cold always creeps in.

All around, the monotonous hum of the call center continues. A tedious symphony of ringing phones and customer service voices. Normally, I resent the company's open floor plan, giving each of us only a tiny cubby of a desk rather than a full office. Yet right now it feels soothing to be nothing more than a cog in a machine. Nobody notices a cog.

I finish the call and stare at the phone on my desk, willing it to ring again so I can start up the script and forget about everything else.

Instead, I hear my name. My fake name, at least.

"Gwen?"

Recognizing my boss's voice, I plaster on a smile before I turn my chair to face him. "Yes?"

Brad is always difficult to read with that perpetual, plasticky grin. But there's a slight furrow between his bushy brows now.

"I've got a personal call for you in my office."

It takes effort to maintain my smile. Alarm bells ring in the back of my mind. There is no one—*no one*—who would have any good reason to contact me here. I have no family. I keep my "friends" at arm's length. None of them would call me at work, even for an emergency. But I can't admit that to my boss without bringing up more questions. Nor can I run for the exit like my instincts are telling me to.

"Okay," I chirp, and follow Brad to his office. He seems in a rush, probably annoyed about me receiving a personal call in the workplace. Little does he know, that phone is practically a shotgun aimed in my direction.

Brad stands by, arms folded over his barrel chest as he looks between me and the phone. He doesn't even have the grace to give me privacy. I'm screaming internally, but there's nothing to do except pick up the phone and hold it to my ear.

"Yes?" I ask.

"Daisy Dumont?"

My stomach plummets. I turn my back to my boss so he doesn't see the blood drain from my face. My voice is suddenly gone, along with any hope that this is a mistake. It's been years since I heard my real name.

"I think you have the wrong number," I say, the words quavering despite my effort to maintain my chipper work façade. I should hang up. Hang up now. But if this call is coming from where I think it's coming from, it's too late. They've already found me. I was foolish to think I could shake them off my trail forever.

"My name is Ezra Bradford," the man on the other side says, ignoring my attempt to disengage. "I'm calling from the Melsbach Research Facility."

All of my worst fears realized. I squeeze my eyes shut. My throat is too tight to speak; I can barely suck in air. But after a stretch of uncomfortable silence on the line, I force myself to turn to my boss.

"Can I have a minute, please?"

Brad must notice the wobble in my lower lip, because his

expression shifts from annoyance to discomfort. "All right," he says, and leaves, shutting the door behind him.

I cup my hand around the receiver. "Listen. I did everything I was supposed to do. You said I would be left alone!" My voice cracks, and I stop.

"Daisy," the man—Ezra—says, gentler than before. "You're not in any trouble. I'm sorry, I should've led with that."

The apology keeps me from hanging up the phone. No one else in *that place* has ever apologized to me for anything. But it still doesn't quash the terror sending shards of ice through my chest.

"This is about Subject X-15," Ezra continues. "I think you know him as Dorian."

Dorian.

My heart cracks open. Even now, the name is enough to bring up a dangerous surge of emotions—pain, longing, loneliness. An ache that has never quite gone away lifts to the surface.

I swallow hard, wet my lips. "Dorian's not real," I whisper, forcing the words out through a tight throat.

There's silence on the other end of the line. Then, "I know that's what they told you to say. I'm sorry you've been forced to pretend it's the truth. But we both know it's not."

I squeeze my eyes shut. This is a trap. A test. It must be. "Dorian was just a way for me to cope with the death of my parents," I say. "He was my childhood imaginary friend."

"Daisy…" Uncertainty leaks into the voice on the phone. "You don't really believe that, do you?"

I have to believe it. Because if I don't, then…

Panic jolts through me, and I hang up.

Chapter Two

After a quick excuse to Brad, I rush to my apartment and pack my things.

My life is, by design, easy to uproot. My meager belongings fit neatly into a single suitcase. I won't be sorry to say goodbye to the little studio apartment I rent month-to-month. I'll email my resignation to work. Brad will be angry, but it doesn't matter. It's not as though I'll be using him as a reference. The moment I received that phone call, I knew I was going to have to shed the persona of Gwen Bailey like I've shed so many before.

I should head out the door the second I'm done. But instead, I hesitate, thinking about that phone call and the past I've tried so hard to forget.

I pace grooves into the ugly, beige carpet. My fingers keep digging into my wrist, scratching at the skin where a hospital bracelet once sat.

But I'm not like that anymore. I don't need the doctors and the pills and the white walls to tell me what's real and what's not. I don't need them to tell me that the monster who lurked under my bed was a figment of my imagination. That Dorian was a way for me to cope with the real monsters of my childhood.

Including my parents, and whoever killed them.

I worked so hard to bury it. To build myself a new and normal life, far from padded rooms and monsters in the darkness and a research facility deep in the Arizona desert.

Don't speak of it. Don't even think of it. I did my best to follow the rules I set for myself, and yet somehow, the past caught up to me anyway.

After I'm done gnawing my fingernails to stubs, I sit with my laptop and type with shaking fingers: *Melsbach Research Facility.*

As usual, a blank page stares back at me. *No results found.* The facility doesn't exist online, or in maps of Ash Valley. By all measures, it's not real. Just like everybody told me. But that phone call…that phone call was real. And the man on the other end spoke like Dorian was real, too.

I type in the name he gave me: *Ezra Bradford.* And there he is. Real.

It isn't hard to find information on him—including an address in Ash Valley, Arizona, and a phone number with a familiar area code.

I stare until the words blur.

I've spent so long trying to convince myself that Dorian was a figment of my imagination. But if Dorian is real, then that means he really was taken by those men in suits with the MRF logo on their clipboards. It means I abandoned him all of those years ago.

If there's even a chance that's true, I can't run from this. I have to try to make things right.

I call Ezra with a burner phone I keep for emergencies.

"Ezra speaking."

"Why did you call me?"

A brief pause on the other end, and then, "Daisy?" he asks.

I drum my fingers on my laptop keyboard. My thoughts are a mess. "D-Dorian," I say, nearly choking on the name. It's been so long since I let myself say it, let myself even *think* about him. He's not real, he can't be real…but I can't fight the surge of emotions every time his name comes up. "Is… Is he…?" I don't even know what I'm trying to ask.

"He's… I'm not sure 'alive' is the right word, but he's still here."

Relief shudders out of me even as I struggle to wrap my mind around this. No one at the MRF ever called Dorian *him* when they interrogated me. They always said "it," or "the subject," or "this so-called friend." They never talked about him like he was real.

Ezra clears his throat. "The reason I called is that we—the MRF—are under new leadership and taking a fresh approach to things. We've been going through our files, reevaluating our subjects in addition to our protocols. X-15—*Dorian*, that is—is a particularly interesting case, especially given his connection to you."

The silence stretches while I try to work up the courage to say something.

"But how did you find me?" I manage. "I've changed my name three times. I've been all over the country. You went through all of the trouble to find me? To contact me at work?"

"I… well… It wasn't me *personally* that…" Another pause, this one almost guilty.

"The MRF has known where I am the entire time," I say, realizing.

"The MRF has some strong feelings about loose ends," he says. "But I didn't contact you on a whim. I know you've been through a lot, Daisy. And so has he. So the reason I'm calling to ask is… Well. Do you want to come see Dorian?"

I stop breathing.

It's a trick. A trap. It has to be. When they took Dorian from me, I asked so many times to be allowed to speak to him. I begged, cried, pleaded. They always said the same thing: "It's a figment of your imagination, a way to deal with the trauma..."

When I persisted, they had me committed.

He's not real. He's not real. He's not real.

"I..." My voice is barely more than a whisper. "I don't... I can't..."

A vague memory stirs. A record spinning. Running through the hallways of my home with a larger, heavier set of footsteps following mine. There's a dull pain behind my eyes, a nameless ache in my chest.

I spent so long convincing myself that he was a coping mechanism, a false memory. But the yearning never went away. I've spent so many nights curled up in bed, crying over something I can't name. Is it possible to miss someone who never existed?

My thoughts are a jagged, painful jumble. But my emotions tug toward home for the first time in seven years.

But that means returning to Ash Valley. To the house. To being *Daisy*.

"I understand this must be strange and sudden, but I could use your help," Ezra says on the other end of the line. "Something is wrong with Dorian, and I'm afraid we don't have much time. You may not have another chance to see him."

I can practically hear the metal jaws of a trap snapping shut around me. Even as I will myself to hang up, I know he's caught me with something impossible to refuse.

If there's the smallest chance that Dorian is real, that he *needs* me, then I can't possibly stay away. This could be my one opportunity to find out the truth about everything that happened.

I shut my eyes and take a deep breath. "What can I do?"

"It's easier to explain in person. When's the soonest you can come?"

I hesitate. "I'll need some time to wrap things up at work. Next weekend?"

"Of course."

We exchange information. I let him buy me a plane ticket. I promise to be there over the weekend.

Then I hang up and head to my already packed car. If I drive without stopping, it will take me about twenty-four hours.

I won't run from this. But I refuse to follow blindly where the MRF leads. They chose to summon me with a phone call instead of sending men in black suits to collect me by force, so perhaps there's some truth in what Ezra said over the phone. Perhaps they've changed.

Perhaps.

But before I go to the MRF, I want to go home, for the first time since my parents were murdered there.

Chapter Three

The sun feels different in Arizona. When I step out of the car, I stop, tilt my head back, and shut my eyes to focus on the sunlight on my face. I know most people hate the desert heat, but I missed it. I'm always cold. I wish it were summertime so I could truly bathe in it, enjoy one of those long, heavy, heat-soaked days...

I've felt starved of sunlight for seven years now, since the last time I saw this house. I was eighteen years old and scared out of my mind. Now I'm twenty-five and...well, I suppose not much has changed.

I roll my shoulders back, stretching out my spine. I ended up stopping a few times along the journey here, catching quick naps on the side of the road and taking care of necessities. But I still made it here far ahead of when the MRF expects me, and that's a comfort. Now I have some space to think, and reaccustom myself to the house.

All this time, and I've never stopped carrying the key. I remove it from my purse as I turn to face the place and stop in shock.

In my head, my childhood home was perfectly preserved, like it was yanked straight out of my memory. But in reality, the place is falling apart after years of neglect. I feel a pinch of something like guilt as I eye the overgrown yard and sagging front porch, the peeling blue paint and grimy windows.

I used to think this place looked like a castle, a beautiful old Queen Anne painted sky-blue, with its pitched roofs and the tower my old room is in.

Yet life here was no fairy tale. And now, it's like looking at the corpse of someone I once knew, rendered unrecognizable by its uncanny stillness.

I shake off that morbid thought and approach the door, each step creaking beneath me as I climb onto the porch. There's something unsettling about this place, to be sure. But it's haunted by nothing more than my old memories now.

Cobwebs gather in the corners and dust coats the furniture. It looks ancient and abandoned. It smells like it, too. Yet a few quick tests prove the electricity and water are still on. The heating system starts with a groan and a stink like something is burning. The utilities and property taxes are still under my bank account, fed by my inheritance so I never have to think about them.

I swallow past a lump in my throat as I turn in a circle to survey the state of things. This place holds many bad memories, but still—it was *home*. Something I haven't had in an awfully long time. That home I remember is still here, it must be. It's just that it's buried beneath seven years of dust and grime. So despite the bone-aching exhaustion of driving with hardly any sleep, I head to the bathroom to find cleaning supplies.

I pause there, wiping a hand over the mirror to reveal my reflection. I try to remember how it felt to be Daisy. I've shed old names and started over like this before, but it's different now that I'm returning to my real name. I try it out a couple times, "Daisy, Daisy" under my breath, but it reminds me of an old song I've tried to forget, so I stop.

Maybe I look the same: lank white-blonde hair, big blue eyes, pale skin. When I was a child, my mother said I looked like a doll. But nowadays, I'm more like an eerie porcelain one than a Barbie, with those shadows under my eyes. It's hard to look at myself for too long.

I shudder, tie back my hair, and bend down to look for those cleaning supplies. They're expired, but they're the best I can hope for.

I spend my first day home cleaning. I move through the foyer to the kitchen, to the dining room and the bathroom, the living room with its vaulted ceiling, my childhood bedroom. The only rooms I leave untouched are my parents' bedroom and the attic. I dust and sweep, mop and scrub and polish, until my back aches and my eyes burn from the chemical vapors. I get filthier as the house gets cleaner, but there is a sense of cleansing my mind as well.

By the time it's done, the sun is setting, and I blink as though I'm emerging from a dream. Or an exorcism. I feel thoroughly wrung out in mind and body.

Despite my work, the house still feels unfamiliar. I know the real issue, though I didn't want to admit it to myself. The problem isn't the dust or even the time that's passed.

The problem is that it feels *empty*. The longer I listen to the silence, the hollower I feel.

I have an urge to clean more, to clean *deeper* despite my sore muscles. But I'm exhausted, and it's late. I need to sleep— but first, my stomach cramps remind me that I should eat something.

Which means going into town.

The thought of being out in public in Ash Valley, being around *people* who might recognize me from my youth, terrifies me. But I need to face my fears sooner or later, and surely nothing can be worse than suffocating slowly in this empty house.

I head into the heart of the town, and circle a local grocery shop twice before finding the courage to go in. But though I've seen a number of familiar places today, there are—thankfully—no familiar faces. I buy enough food to survive for a few days and some fresh flowers to brighten up the place. Then I hurry home.

Home. How odd that I'm thinking of it that way already. But in reality, my childhood home was the only one I ever had. Every other apartment I've lived in has just been a temporary place to hide.

When I arrive back at the house, a dead bird waits for me on the porch. Black and white and blue feathers mark the fragile little body. I remember a flash of similar colors when the bird hit my window at work, all the way back in Seattle, and disquiet curls in my stomach. Another magpie. *Two for joy,* goes the saying, but somehow I know there's more to come.

I try to tell myself that it's idle superstition, something I thought I rid myself of a long time ago, but I can't shake my anxiety. After I carry the groceries inside, I return to wrap the tiny, almost weightless body in a plastic bag, laying him to the most dignified rest I can grant right now. I whisper an apology as I tuck it into the garbage bin. Maybe this isn't my fault, but it feels like it might be.

Once I'm inside, I lock the door behind me. If I was hoping for a sense of safety here, I don't find it. The house still feels odd, like a stranger who looks like someone you used to know. But I find a vase for the flowers and simmer some water with cinnamon sticks and orange peels till the smell of it permeates the musk. I eat the sandwich I grabbed at the store and make myself a pot of herbal tea, and then I feel more grounded. Hopefully, enough to sleep. It's never come easily to me.

As I step into my bedroom, I pause, staring at faded pencil marks on the doorway. One side says *Daisy*. Each tick has a year next to it, marking my height as it slowly rises from a child's size to my current stature.

The other side says *Dorian*. The marks start around the same place as mine did, but the last one is so high, I have to stretch my arm to touch it.

Nostalgia is a dull ache in my chest. But there's another feeling, too. Something strange I can't quite identify.

Shaking it off, I step into my room and run my hand over the creamy off-white sheets of my bed, stopping behind the chair to my vanity table. I have a vivid rush of memory—sitting here, combing my hair, carefully arranging ribbons in it while looking in the mirror—and ache to do so again, but my overworked muscles argue otherwise. Instead, I turn around, hesitate, and lower myself to my knees on the hardwood floor. I lean over and peek under the bed.

There's nothing there, of course. But at one corner, I find the familiar sight of letters scratched into the wood. D-A-I-S-Y, carved in crude markings. I run my fingertips over them and smile.

"Good night," I whisper to the nothing beneath my bed, and climb under the covers.

Sadness comes, as it so often does. Silent tears trickling down my cheeks, turning to body-wracking sobs. There is an ache in my chest I cannot name. I want... I *want*.

This mattress was always too big for me. But it's as soft as I remember, and eventually, sleep arrives. As I drift away, I can almost imagine the warmth of another, larger body wrapped around mine.

15

Chapter Four

The rest of the week passes in a blur. I clean and wander the empty halls and reacquaint myself with the house. I avoid the attic and try not to stare at the floorboards at the bottom of the stairs. Is there still a reddish tinge to the wood, or is it my imagination?

Just as I've built myself a safe place, I'm forced to leave it, because soon arrives the day I'm supposed to go to the Melsbach Research Facility.

My stomach ties itself into knots at the thought. There's an itch under my skin, a nervous hum in my bones. Untapped energy with nowhere to go. I prefer to hide away when I feel like this, but I can't when they're dangling the promise of Dorian in front of me.

Dorian, Dorian. I've been trying so hard not to think his name or see his face in the empty corners of the house. I can't remember the last time I allowed myself to hope for something. And there's still a steady chant in the back of my mind—*not real, not real, not real*. It sounds like my parents, my psychiatrist, the MRF, and I still don't know if I can trust my own voice above theirs.

I tremble through the entire drive over to that horrible, stark facility on the edge of town, and barely manage to squeak my name out to the security guard at the gate. When he calls in to the facility on the radio, I'm certain I'm about to be swarmed by men in suits. But the guard waves me through, and I walk inside. Right into the jaws of the waiting beast.

"Daisy?" I flinch. I'm still getting used to the idea of fitting myself into that name again. A young man approaches me. "I'm Ezra Bradford. Thank you for coming."

Ezra is barely older than I am, reedy and nonthreatening despite his considerable height. His eyes are kind behind his black-rimmed glasses. His tie has dinosaurs on it. I stare at it; the MRF I remember isn't the kind of place where men wearing dinosaur ties work.

"Thank you so much for coming here," he says, and holds out a hand. "I know this must have been difficult."

He doesn't mention the fact that I was supposed to be at the airport this morning and wasn't.

I bite the inside of my cheek and accept his hand. As our fingers brush, a strange feeling zips through me—some mixture of a static shock and an intense sense of déjà vu.

Ezra drops my hand and looks as taken aback as I feel. "Have we met before?" he asks, flexing his fingers before sliding them into his pocket.

"I don't think so." I'm certain we haven't, but for a moment, it felt like I *knew* him. An instant connection. Not romantic, but the way I'd imagine I'd feel if I met some long-lost relative or someone I knew in a past life. But I shake it off.

"Could we step into my office?" Ezra asks.

I want to remind him he promised I could see Dorian. But saying it out loud will be as good as admitting I no longer believe he's *not real.* I glance over my shoulder at the exit, and then back at Ezra. The silence hangs between us.

"My hope is that the better I understand him, the better care I can provide," Ezra says.

The corners of my mouth twitch downward. *Care*, he calls it? I desperately want to retreat, but I can't. I need to be brave. "Okay."

Ezra guides me toward a bearded man in a security uniform. My eyes dart from his name tag—*Hunter Barnes*—to the scar that cuts across his cheek, and finally to my shoes.

"Barnes, this is the temp I mentioned," Ezra says. "She's here to consult on Subject X-15."

I note the use of "X-15" instead of "Dorian," like he's been saying to me. The knot of anxiety in my gut winds tighter.

The security guard checks his clipboard. "Got it. You're good to go."

We step through the metal detector, and Ezra scans his ID card to open the door leading into the facility. He holds the door open for me.

I hesitate at the doorway, glancing over my shoulder once more, and force myself to step through.

The fluorescent lights, the too-white walls, the endless metal doors… I've never been to this place, but I've had nightmares that started like this. It reminds me of the mental hospital. My palms sweat as Ezra leads me through the halls. He stops in front of a door and I clasp my hands to hide their trembling.

His office is surprisingly cozy. A bookshelf in one corner holds a medley of books on ghost hunting and paranormal experiences, along with a Boba Fett figurine and an oversized D20. A coffee mug with an image of a cactus and the words "Don't be a prick" holds pens on his desk.

It's hard to connect someone like Ezra to the MRF agents I

met on that night seven years ago. Still, I sit on the edge of the chair he offers, ready to bolt for the door if necessary. Across the desk from me, Ezra opens a folder and grabs a pen.

My stomach curdles with dread, already anticipating the questions he's going to ask. One question in particular. I already have the answer ready: *I don't remember.*

But instead Ezra says, "First off, let me tell you about me."

I blink in surprise.

"I work with a variety of subjects here," he continues. "Generally with those classified as ghosts or spirits. Dorian shares some common traits with them. The invisibility and incorporeality, the fact that he can be confined with salt and iron, that all aligns with what I know about ghosts."

I used to wonder how they managed to capture and trap Dorian…until I stopped wondering and started telling myself he was never real. My mind is still ping-ponging between the two beliefs. I sit with my hands folded in my lap, trying not to squirm.

"My initial theory was that he was a poltergeist," Ezra continues. "That checked out when I looked into the history of your house." He passes a folder over to me, with an old newspaper clipping sitting on top. There's a faded image of a somber, dark-haired young boy. My stomach flips as I look into his familiar eyes. "That's Dorian Elwood. His family lived in the house before yours, and he disappeared when he was about ten."

I can't take my eyes off the picture. He looks familiar…and yet not. I remember the pencil marks on my doorway, which began at my size as a child and grew so much taller.

"Poltergeists are usually the ghosts of murdered children, their hauntings intense but brief. But Dorian has been around for seven years in our custody alone, and he doesn't behave like a child."

I can feel Ezra's eyes on me, but I keep my gaze firmly on the desk between us. He hasn't asked any questions yet, so I don't speak; I haven't decided how much I'm willing to tell him, anyway. I'm still afraid he'll suddenly swap from talking about him like this to insisting that Dorian never existed, just like the MRF agents did seven years ago.

"Even with poltergeists, I've never seen a spirit that can interact with the physical world as much as he does," Ezra continues. Then he pauses. "Or at least, as much as he did."

My stomach drops, and I finally lift my eyes to meet his. "What do you mean?"

"Dorian is fading," he says. "When I first started working here, he was notably corporeal most of the time. He would interact with objects in the room frequently and react to various stimuli. But now days go by without any activity." He looks from his notes to me. "It's natural for ghosts to pass on eventually. Normally, I'd encourage it. But when I read his file, I wanted to make sure you had a chance to see him first."

I can only stare at him, my face stricken. I'm imagining what would've happened if I hadn't picked up that call or agreed to come here. What if Dorian had faded away into nonexistence before I had a chance to see him? My stomach clenches with dread; the emotion is stronger than that persistent whisper in my head that all of this is a lie. I need to see him. I need to know that he *does* exist, even if it's only for a chance to say goodbye.

"Please," I say, my voice trembling. "Can I talk to him?"

Ezra nods. "Yes, but I should warn you, his behavior has been erratic—"

"I'm not afraid of Dorian." That has *always* been the truth.

"It's been years since you last saw him," Ezra says. "He may not be the same as you remember."

My instinct is always to nod and agree, to keep my head down, to make myself as small and nonthreatening as possible. But I force myself to speak up now, even though my hands are trembling in my lap. "You promised me I could see him."

Ezra hesitates. "You can," he says. "But— I'm sorry, I can't let you into his holding cell. I wish I could, but we recently had an incident with a subject escaping with a hostage. Security is on edge. And given Dorian's history…"

He looks at me like he's expecting me to refute it, but I look away. I breathe in and out, keeping a lid on my emotions. "Then why did you bring me here?" I ask.

"I can't let you into the room," Ezra says, "but I can still let you talk to him."

Chapter Five

My heart beats a wild rhythm as I step into the observation room. My eyes dart around to take in details—the plain metal desk and single chair, the control system with its intercom and various buttons—before stopping on the window into the next room. Ezra hangs back as I approach it, my trembling hands clasped into fists at my sides.

On the other side of the window sits an empty room. Dorian's cell. It's a tiny, plain box with white walls and tile. There are no windows other than this one, and only a single door. The only furniture is a cot in one corner and a metal table and chair, all welded to the floor. A coloring book and some crayons are scattered across the table. On the floor, a teddy bear's head sits facing the viewing window; the rest of its body is nowhere to be found.

Ezra clears his throat from behind me.

"Like I said, I was operating under the assumption he was a poltergeist at first. Thus the toys. I wanted to see if he'd play like a child's ghost would."

I stare at the decapitated teddy bear. Its beady black eyes stare back. "I'm guessing he wasn't pleased."

"That's one way to put it."

I laugh despite my nerves, but it turns into a sob halfway up my throat. I press the back of my hand to my mouth and shut my eyes. Seeing that tiny room makes the gravity of this situation weigh on my shoulders. If it's true, if he is *real*, like Ezra is telling me, it means Dorian has been trapped here for years. Years without a glimpse of the sun, without anything but children's toys to amuse himself with.

I left Ash Valley and never looked back. And all of this time, he's been trapped here.

"Can he see through the glass?" I ask, my throat tight.

"Right now it's transparent, yes."

I take a shuddery breath and nod. "Can he hear me?"

Ezra steps up to the control panel.

"Once I hit the intercom button, he'll be able to," Ezra says. "Are you ready?"

I nod. Ezra flashes an *okay* sign.

Now that the time has come, I'm not sure what to say. I lean closer to the window, struggling to form words. "Dorian?" I ask, my voice cracking. "It's me, Daisy. I know it's been a very long time, but I… I'm here."

I search the room on the other side of the window, but there's nothing. I swallow a lump in my throat and fight back the tears pricking my eyes.

"Please, talk to me," I say, desperation leaking into my tone. "Show yourself. Give me a sign. Anything…"

Show me that you're real.

As I stand there, hand pressed against the glass, I wonder if it's already too late. I don't realize I'm trembling until Ezra touches my shoulder. I suck in a breath, wipe my eyes, and turn to him. "Is he gone?"

Ezra holds up a small device. It looks almost like a radiation detector, but with glowing lights that are currently shifting between green and yellow and back again.

"This is an EMF reader," Ezra says. "It monitors electromagnetic fields. Most hauntings give off energy fluctuations. It's reacting now, so he's responding to your presence, but…"

As I lean in to look, the EMF reader spikes to orange. I step back, and it recedes.

Ezra is focused on the viewing window. "I'm not seeing any activity, but he's definitely reacting." He taps a display on the desk. "Temperature is dropping, too, which is another classic sign of a spirit's presence. He's there. He heard you."

I bite my lip, fighting frustration. "I don't understand why he won't appear to me, then."

Ezra looks up at me. "Are you saying you used to be able to *see* him?"

I glance away, face heating. I was determined not to say too much, especially not anything that would make me seem different or weird, but it seems I've already blown it. "Um…"

"He might be too weak to manifest right now," Ezra says, instead of pressing further.

Or he hates me. Or he was never real in the first place—

I gulp back the threat of further tears and force myself to nod. "Is there anything I can do to help?"

"Yes, actually, there might be." Ezra stares into the cell, arms folded across his chest. "Spirits often lose themselves— and eventually fade entirely—when they're forgotten. But it strengthens them to be acknowledged. To hear their names and things about their life. If you spend time with Dorian, talk to him, share what you remember, maybe there's a way for you to remind him who he is."

The thought of diving into our shared past, our secrets, *that night*, makes me sick to my stomach. I stare down at my shoes, unable to form a response. My heart says *yes*, but the rest of me is so, so afraid.

Ezra says quietly, "I'm not going to force you to do anything you don't want to do, Daisy. If you want to go, you're free to go. I'll erase your name from our files, and no one from the MRF will ever bother you again. I swear it." I look up at him, startled. His expression is open and earnest, begging me to trust him, but I don't know if I can.

Especially not if he intends to dredge up the past that I've tried so hard to forget. It will be an immense risk, uncovering all that I've hidden. For a terrifying moment, I imagine myself trapped in a cell just like the one on the other side of the glass. Padded walls and a straitjacket. Electrodes strapped to my head and needles in my veins. I shiver. I lived through my stint in the mental hospital, but there are worse—and more permanent—fates.

And yet if Ezra is correct, this is my only chance to make things right.

"Maybe it's time for him to pass on," Ezra continues. "I wanted to give you a chance to say goodbye, but if you think that's what's best—"

"*No*," I burst out. The reaction is immediate, visceral—every fiber of my being screams against the notion. I slowly lift my eyes to meet Ezra's. "I want to try to talk to him. Where do we start?"

He studies me and dips his chin in a nod. "With the beginning, I suppose."

* * *

Ezra finds another chair, and soon he and I sit facing each other in the observation room, a few feet away from the viewing panel that shows Dorian's cell. The intercom is still lit, so if he's there, he can hear everything.

The setup is strange, almost formal, like a job interview. Or an interrogation. My palms sweat where I've jammed them in my lap, and my leg jumps, tapping an anxious beat against the tile.

"There's no need to be nervous," Ezra says. "We're just having a conversation. Maybe Dorian will react, or maybe he won't. Either way, we'll learn something. Yes?"

"I understand." But that doesn't stop my heart from thumping.

Ezra sets a tape recorder on the table next to us. "Is it all right for me to record this conversation? It's for my personal notes only."

"Okay."

He hits the button.

"This is Ezra Bradford of the MRF, session one with Subject X-15 and visitor Daisy Dumont," he says. "Today's goal is to establish the basic history of X-15 and Dumont and see if the subject has any reaction to her presence and the memories she chooses to share."

I glance at the recorder, the viewing panel, and then down at my clasped hands.

"How did you first become acquainted with X-15?" Ezra asks.

"It started with the scratching," I say, barely a whisper. He leans forward, trying to hear better, and I raise my voice. "A scratching sound under my bed every night."

"How old were you?" Ezra asks.

"Um…maybe eight," I say. He nods for me to go on, and I clear my throat. "The scratching kept happening. Every night, like clockwork, at midnight."

"Repetitive behavior," Ezra mutters. "Probably—" He glances at me, catches himself. "Sorry. Continue. Were you scared of the sound?"

"At first, I hid under my covers. But when it kept happening, I thought maybe it was an animal. A mouse. Something I could keep as a pet. I tried to lure it out with cheese. When that didn't work, one night I climbed to the edge of the bed and looked underneath."

Even after years of trying to suppress it, I can remember that moment with striking clarity. The hummingbird thrum of my heartbeat, the way my hair fell around my head as I lowered it, upside-down, to look.

"It was hard to see…" The lights were off, and I had only the dim glow of moonlight coming through the window. "But there was…something. A silhouette hunched under the bed. Not an animal." As I talk, it comes more into focus in my mind. I'm shocked at how clearly I remember it. My psychiatrist probably would've said it was because I've told myself the story so many times, I started to believe it. I falter at the thought, but Ezra gives me an encouraging nod that spurs me onward.

"I saw something humanoid. Just a little bigger than me. Hunched on his hands and knees, with a crooked head staring back at me." My lips lift in a wry smile. "*Then* I was scared. I recoiled back into bed and screamed so loud that my parents came running. But of course, when they turned on the lights and went to look, the figure was gone. Instead, they found letters carved into the wood under my bed: D-A-I-S-Y."

"Interesting." Ezra leans back in his chair, his expression thoughtful. "He was your size. So he *was* a child. And with a physical manifestation… Anyway, continue. Did you try to tell your parents what you had seen?"

"Yes, but they didn't believe me." I fiddle with my hands, tracing the crooks in my pinky and ring fingers. "My parents tore the room apart trying to find whatever sharp object I had used to carve my name, but they found nothing." I shrug. "They took away my books to punish me. They thought reading too close to bed was giving me an overactive imagination." Or so they said. Really, I think, it was the cruelest thing they could think of. "But the scratching continued. I would just lie awake in the darkness, petrified, listening to that sound every night and imagining the figure I had seen. It frightened me so badly that it knew my name. It meant that it was there more often than I thought, listening…"

"Did he try to come out again? To interact with you at all?"

I shake my head. "He stayed under the bed. I think he realized that I was scared. Or maybe he was scared too. I don't know." I shrug. "We went on like that for about a week. Then one day I was lying in bed, listening to that scratching again, thinking about how he was stuck under there every night all alone. And I thought—" I swallow. "I thought he must be lonely."

Loneliness was something I knew all too well, even as a child. I knew it so deeply and so horribly that I could not help but empathize, even with a monster.

So that night I crept out from beneath the covers. I put my socked feet on the floorboards, one at a time. Goose bumps rippled all over my skin as I anticipated a sudden grab, a flash of claws. But it didn't come. Even the scratching had gone silent.

"I crept over to my closet, knelt down, and rummaged around until I found what I was looking for," I murmur. "A toy. A rubber ball. I sat cross-legged on the floor with my back against the wall, far enough away that I couldn't quite see the corner under the bed. Still, it was like I could *feel* something there, watching me."

Ezra is silent now, watching me with the same intense attention I remember from that moment.

"Very carefully, I rolled the ball under the bed," I say. "And then it rolled back, just as gently, and bumped against my foot. And I smiled. I said—" I pause, biting my lip. "I said, 'Hello, my name is Daisy.' Judging from the scratches, he already knew, but I figured it couldn't hurt to be polite." I swallow and raise my eyes to Ezra's again. "And then a bloodied hand came out from the darkness." Slowly, cautiously. "And he waved at me."

Chapter Six

I wake up in the middle of the night to the sound of music. A half-familiar melody drifts into my cracked door from the hallway. It seems to fill the emptiness of the house, creeping into every open space. It's a cheerful song, and by the time it reaches the chorus, it's easy to remember the name. "Run, Rabbit, Run!"

It's jaunty and playful…and I'm paralyzed in bed, my heart thumping almost painfully hard. The terror is bone-deep and inexplicable, and I stay there, clutching my sheets to my chest, until the music fades and I drift into sleep again.

By the time morning arrives, I'm certain it was just a dream. But when I walk downstairs, I find that the vase of flowers I bought the other day—which were perfectly fine until last night—have blackened and withered.

When I find a third dead magpie waiting on my porch, I'm barely even surprised.

* * *

It's a little easier to walk into the MRF the next morning,

knowing that they let me walk out once. Although Dorian didn't react to the story I told yesterday, Ezra seemed optimistic and encouraged me to come in again as soon as I was able. It isn't like I have much to do in Ash Valley, so today I'm back bright and early to try again.

But when I see Ezra waiting for me in the lobby, his face is drawn and his eyebrows knotted.

I stop short, fear jolting through me. "What happened?"

"Well…" He grimaces. "We asked for a sign yesterday, and we got one."

"That's good, right?" I ask, unsure why he seems so tense. "That's what we wanted?"

"I'm not so sure. Come and see."

Ezra leads me back into the observation room. We stand in front of the viewing window as he opens the metal shutters and shows me Dorian's cell.

My breath catches in my throat.

DAISY DAISY DAISY DAISY DAISY
DAISY DAISY DAISY DAISY DAISY
DAISY DAISY DAISY DAISY DAISY

My name is written all over the white walls. A hundred silent screams. More. What remains of his crayons are tiny, broken nubs scattered on the tile.

I turn slowly, taking it all in. My lips pull into a trembling smile because this is a sign that Dorian is here. That he's *real* in a way nobody can deny. But when I turn to Ezra, he's staring at me instead of the room, his expression troubled.

"Doesn't this frighten you?"

I blink, surprised by the question. "Why would it? This is what we wanted."

Ezra bites his thumbnail, glancing through the window again.

"Like I said, sometimes spirits lose themselves. They can warp into something…malevolent. The longer they stay, the worse it becomes. That's why I usually aid them in passing on." He looks back at me. "Is there any chance that Dorian could be holding a grudge?"

I open my mouth, shut it again. Look back at the room and all those etchings of my name. A grudge? It doesn't feel right to me. I spoke honestly yesterday when I said I've never been afraid of Dorian.

But it's been seven years. Years I've abandoned him, denied his existence. I've spent so much time telling myself he isn't real that even now, with this evidence in front of me, I am afraid to believe otherwise.

"I need to see him," I say, both to myself and to Ezra. "If you would just let me go in there…" Yet I already know what Ezra's answer will be. Any chance I had of seeing Dorian went out the window with this incident. *Why?* I plead silently, staring into the cell.

"I think it's important, before we continue, to have a full understanding of what we're dealing with here." Dread unfurls in my stomach at his words. I already know what's coming, the words I've been anticipating ever since I arrived here. "We need to talk about what happened that night."

That night. My mind recoils. My breath quickens.

"I need more time," I say. "Please. Look, I understand your concern. I won't ask to enter the room again until I tell you everything, but—" I swallow hard, shake my head. "I'm not ready to talk about what happened to my parents yet."

Ezra is silent for a few long moments. His eyes and his judgment weigh on me even as I stare down at my shoes. Anxious energy hisses under my skin. My hands form fists at my sides, fingernails digging into the tender skin of my palms as I try to steady myself.

Finally, he sighs. "I understand it must be a sensitive subject," he says. "We need to talk about it eventually, because I suspect that our files don't tell the full truth. But for now, let's proceed as we did yesterday. *Carefully.*"

I can see his confidence faltering. But that's okay, because he's giving me—giving Dorian—a chance. I'm certain there's still a way to earn Ezra's trust and make this work. "Thank you," I whisper, and take a seat at the table.

Ezra sits too, after a last, lingering glance through the viewing window. He sets up the tape recorder and hits the button that will allow our conversation to play over the intercom into the cell.

"This is Ezra Bradford, session two with Subject X-15 and visitor Daisy Dumont," he says, shuffling his papers on the desk. "Welcome back, Daisy. And hello, X-15; I can see you've tried communicating with us."

"Hi, Dorian," I say softly, my eyes flicking to the window.

We both pause, but there's no sign of a response. Dorian still doesn't appear. I swallow my disappointment. I suspected it wouldn't be that easy, but still, I'm desperate to see him.

"Before we jump in today, I wanted to ask if you had any suggestions for ways we could help X-15 talk to us," Ezra says. "He's trying to reach out. I'd like to do anything we can to make that easier for him."

I chew my lip, considering. My mind wanders to that dream—was it a dream?—I had last night, and the half-familiar song drifting through the halls of my old house. "He's always liked music."

Ezra nods. "I could see if I can get approval to bring in

something for him."

"Maybe a record player. We used to listen to one in the house."

I can clearly see that old record player spinning, the scratchy sound of a very old tune. What was that song, again? It's right on the tip of my tongue, but I can't seem to recall. I shiver and push the thought away when I realize Ezra is giving me an odd look.

I force a smile. "I'm excited to try."

"Now, tell me about your childhood with Dorian. He stayed in your room after that first contact?"

I nod. "He wouldn't come out from under the bed, though. He said he didn't want me to see his face… I thought he was just shy."

"And your parents?"

I go rigid in my chair. "What about them?"

"Did you tell them about Dorian?"

"Yes. Well, I tried."

"And what did they say?"

"That I was too old to have an imaginary friend." My fingers curl into fists in my lap, my shoulders bracing. "I don't want to talk about my parents."

"Okay. Talk about whatever you want, then."

I tell him the first few things that come to mind. Talking to Dorian every night as I fell asleep, putting my stuffed animals under the bed so he wouldn't be alone when I was out of the house. The more I talk, the more memories come to mind. Small everyday moments that I haven't thought about in years.

A wet warmth on my face surprises me. When I lift my hand to my mouth, I realize it's blood trickling from my nose.

"Oh," I say. "Sorry. It must be the dry air."

"Hang on, I'll go grab you something for that." Ezra pushes

out his chair and heads for the door.

As soon as he leaves me alone in the observation room, I beeline for the window. "Dorian," I whisper, looking into his cell. I bring my fingertips to the window and touch it, straining to see some sign of him in the emptiness. "Are you really here? Talk to me."

Movement flickers in the corner. But before I can focus on it, the door behind me opens again. I turn to face Ezra, and as I pull my hand away from the window, it leaves behind a streak of red.

* * *

Sharing my memories of Dorian doesn't seem to do anything but heighten my grief. My chest and throat are tight by the time we call it a day. And even after I wash the blood off my face, the taste of copper lingers on the back of my tongue.

And the more I remember, the more aware I am that I've been shoving all of this into a corner of my brain for the last seven years. How could I have forgotten so much? How could I have ever left Dorian behind?

When I get home, the house feels emptier than ever. The memory of the record player lingers. Where was it, again? I wander from room to room, searching, until I see the pull string for the attic in the upstairs hallway.

Unease ripples over my skin. Something urges me not to reach for it, not to go up there.

I shake it off and yank the string. A dusty ladder unfolds before me, providing stairs up into darkness. I force myself to put one foot up, and then another. There's nothing to be scared of in this house, I tell myself. Not anymore.

The attic is small enough that I have to hunch when I stand, dustier than the rest of the house, and bitterly cold. Stacks of old boxes line the walls. But as I glance around, familiarity flickers within my mind. A faint memory of passing afternoons up here, lit only by the single small window, listening to music. I must have been up here a million times as a child. It's strange my mind didn't immediately go here when I thought of the record player.

And there it is, sitting in a corner, waiting for me. I blow off a layer of dust and gently lower the tonearm onto the waiting record. A brief pause, and a song begins to play: "Daisy Bell."

I smile at the familiar lyrics, listening to the rich sound of the record. A memory stirs somewhere in my mind, but it slips away before I can grasp it. Instead, I just stand and listen, my eyes shut and my heart at peace, for once.

Chapter Seven

"I wasn't able to get my hands on a good record player on such short notice, but I found this in storage." Ezra holds up an antique radio, polished wood with a brass dial to change the station.

I smile. "I think he'll like it." God, I hope I'm right. I want so badly to see him. This will be our third session at the MRF, and I hope today is the day Dorian will reveal himself.

"I'm going to go put it in his room. You can watch through the window if you'd like."

As badly as I want to accompany him into the cell, I know he'll never say yes until I tell him about *that night*. So I bite my tongue and stand beside the viewing window in the observation room as Ezra goes to give the radio to Dorian.

When the door in the cell opens, I strain to see through to get a better idea of how Dorian is being trapped. *Iron and salt*, Ezra mentioned, but I'm not sure where it is or how it works. All I can see is that Ezra is in a small chamber with another, closed door behind him. Two doors, one of them shut at all times, like an airlock or a quarantine chamber. I watch as Ezra walks inside and sets the radio on the metal table. Nothing in the cell moves, other than Ezra. He walks out, shuts the door behind him, and soon reappears in the observation room with me.

I'm about to speak, but I pause as music starts within the cell. Ezra and I both look through the window at the now lit-up radio. It takes only a couple seconds for me to recognize the same soothing melody I listened to last night: "Daisy Bell."

Delight zips up my spine. *He's here.* I quickly reach over to hit the intercom. "Dorian?" I whisper, peering into the room. I stay quiet, listening and waiting to see if Dorian will appear, but he doesn't. My shoulders sag, and I turn back to Ezra.

"We used to listen to that song all the time on the record player up in the attic," I say. "I went up there last night. I found this." I dig into my pocket and pull out the crumpled paper. It's one of my childhood drawings of us. Me: small, blonde, excited. Him: taller, dark-haired, face hidden behind a white, grinning mask.

Ezra smiles as I show him, but his brow furrows as he takes a closer look. "The mask...?"

"I gave it to him," I say. "Like I mentioned, he never wanted to show his face. He said it would scare me. When I was drawing this picture, I realized I didn't even know what he looked like. So I drew him with a mask. And then all of a sudden he peeked out from beneath the bed, and he was wearing it."

I smile as I remember him crawling out from under the bed, that smiling white mask emerging from the darkness.

"His appearance changed?" Ezra murmurs. "Unusual... But, all right, continue. That's the first time he came out?"

"Yes. I was so excited." That was the first time we sat face-to-face—or face-to-mask, rather—cross-legged on my bedroom floor. I took his hands in mine. "Then I asked him if he wanted gloves, too, because his hands looked like they hurt. They were all…torn up. I asked him what happened to him, to make his hands like that, and then…"

The radio goes staticky within Dorian's cell, the song glitching. *Da-Da-Daisy…*

My brow furrows as the rest of the story evades me. It's like I've hit a wall. There's more to the memory, I know it, but as I reach for it, it slips through my fingers like it never existed at all. "And then… I…" Why can't I remember? I force myself to focus: to remember looking down at Dorian's small hands with his torn fingernails and bloodied fingertips. I can picture him leaning in, whispering as he told me… told me…?

Something important. I can feel it. It's there in my head, I just can't quite…

Disjointed moments flash through my brain. The lights flickering. Eyes in the darkness. Someone screaming. The attic hatch rattling—

I gasp, pressing my palms to my eyes as pain flares in my skull. The song on the radio turns to pure static, but buried within it, I hear a deep, echoing voice whispering my name.

"Daisy?" Ezra's voice seems far away, as if through water. "Are you all right?"

"Yes, I…" I lower my hands, and a drop of red splatters on the table. I raise my hand to my nose and it comes away wet with blood.

Dorian's bloody hands, his eyes sad behind his mask.

"What happened to you?"

I'm right on the verge of remembering more, but my skull is pounding, my heart thumping in terror of… *something.*

Sudden movement out of the corner of my eye jerks me out of my reverie. I lift my head, and my heart skips a beat.

Dorian.

He's here, standing right on the other side of the glass. Visible. *Real.*

I can *see* him, and he is achingly familiar and strangely different at the same time. He's tall and lean, his limbs long and spindly. He must be nearly seven feet now, so tall he has to tilt his head to the side to look through the viewing panel. He has the same washed-out quality I remember, his coloring sepia-toned and his image blurry around the edges like an old photograph. He wears a black suit and a bowtie, like an old-fashioned butler. His skin is covered from his polished boots to his dark gloves, stretched to cover the long, long fingers on all four of his hands.

And of course, he wears his mask. Porcelain and blank, with holes for his eyes and his mouth—the latter stretched into a crude smile, just like the picture I once drew for him.

Our gazes meet. His eyes are wide, almost frantic.

"Dorian!" Possessed by a sudden, frantic *need,* I lurch out of my chair and toward the window, my hand outstretched.

Just before I reach it, Dorian grabs the radio and hurls it toward the glass. I flinch away as it hits the window with a loud *bang,* and by the time I lower my hand from my face and look again, he's gone.

I press my fingers to the glass, searching—but there's nothing but the radio on the floor. Still, I can't stop a smile from spreading across my face, even as tears well up in my eyes.

"Hi, Dorian," I whisper.

He's real. He's really real.

Right? Struck by a sudden need to confirm I wasn't the only one who saw that, I turn to Ezra, who is pale with shock as he stares at the viewing panel.

"That…that was *not* a poltergeist. The size of him…"

My eyes widen. "You saw him too?"

His mouth opens, shuts. "I saw the height the radio was held at. He must be, what, seven feet tall?"

"Something like that." I realize with a lurch how scared Ezra looks. His fingers tremble as he turns off the intercom.

"This is good," I say, desperate for Ezra to see. "He showed himself!"

Ezra's eyebrows pull together, his fear bleeding into incredulity. "He tried to attack us."

"He was just getting our attention! He knew the window wouldn't break."

Ezra shakes his head. "I think this is a mistake," he murmurs. "I thought I knew what I was dealing with here, but I was wrong."

No. Panic wells up inside of me as indecision crosses Ezra's face. "Please don't say that," I say. "This means what we're doing is working. It's making him stronger."

"But it also might be making him dangerous." Ezra stares into the cell at the shattered remains of the radio. Then he slaps the button to close the viewing panel. I resist the urge to protest as the metal shutters close off my view of the room. "I think… I think we should take a break and reevaluate what we're doing."

The panic inside of me swells. I struggle to keep it down, to keep myself under control. I wrap my arms around myself as if I can physically restrain the feeling. "But we don't know how much time we have," I say. "What if he fades while we're *reevaluating?*"

"I want to help him. I do. But not at the expense of your safety or anyone else's."

No. Not now. Dorian is real, I *saw* him, and that glimpse has intensified the ache of his loss tenfold. The panic is a living thing inside of me now, clawing and desperate. It snarls through my chest, climbs up the back of my throat like bile.

Breaking free.

No, no, no.

"You promised me," I whisper.

"I told you I'd give you a chance to say goodbye, and—"

"*No!*"

Anger breaks through the terror gripping me. Something inside of me *cracks,* and the metal table on the other side of the room suddenly lifts into the air before thumping back down, sending Ezra's files scattering all over the floor.

Ezra flinches, staring at it. Then at me.

My jaw drops. I try to speak, but nothing comes out. The anger is gone just as quickly as it arrived, leaving me with nothing but fear and the desire to make myself small and unnoticeable.

But it's too late. Ezra noticed me. The real version of me, which I've been trying so hard to hide.

A shocked silence falls over both of us. Our eyes meet, and I see the realization in his. *He knows.* I open my mouth to say something, make some excuse, but I can't seem to speak. It's been so long since I lost control of my powers like that. I've worked so hard to keep them bottled up. For it to happen now, here, is unthinkable.

What have I done? Now he knows—the MRF's mistake, seven years ago, was not locking me up in a cell just like Dorian. Because I'm a monster, too.

"That…must have been X-15," Ezra says. "Maybe he cracked the glass. Or he's getting too strong for the barriers. I'll have to make the room hasn't been compromised."

I stare at him, still slack-jawed. I should just accept that explanation and the out it gives me, but…but I saw that look in his eyes. He *knows*. So why is he covering for me?

Ezra crosses the room and picks up his notebook from the floor. He looks at the table, at the scattered papers.

I swallow the lump in my throat. "Y-Yes. Sorry, that… I… I'm a bit shocked, I'm sorry."

"Understandable. Are you okay?" Ezra scrawls in his notepad and holds it up.

Play along, it says. I glance at the words and then at his face, uncertain.

"I'm…fine," I say. "Are you?"

"I'm all right." He nods, and scribbles again: *We can't talk here*. He inclines his head toward the camera in the corner, and I realize he's intentionally placed his back toward it so the notebook isn't visible.

"Um. Good. I guess we should probably call it a day." I'm already stepping toward the door, trying not to stare at that camera. Even if Ezra is on my side for some reason, that doesn't mean the MRF will be. I need to go. Now. Leave town and run again before it's too late.

I hate the thought of leaving Dorian behind, but what am I supposed to do? If I stay, I'll just be locked up alongside him.

Ezra lifts a hand as if to stop me but then lowers it. "Right. Of course. But, uh…listen, we're both shaken up, I think. How about we go grab some coffee and talk?"

I pause, caged halfway between him and the door and not sure which is the safer option. Is this some kind of trick designed to keep me here while he calls in backup? What is he playing at?

While I'm still deciding my answer, Ezra writes in the notebook once more and holds it up. When I read the message, time seems to stop.

I am like you, it says.

Chapter Eight

Ezra and I stare at each across the diner table while I drum my fingers on my mug of hot cocoa. My mind is still reeling from the fact that I accidentally revealed myself to him. It's been years since I lost control like that. Maybe being around Dorian has an effect on me…or maybe it's Ezra.

I'm desperate to learn more. If he's truly like me, as he said, how can he hide himself well enough that he can work at the MRF of all places? What do his powers look like? Can he teach me to control mine? I have so many questions, but I'm not sure where to begin.

"I can't believe this place is still open," I say to break the silence. The diner is exactly as I remember it, including the sticky menus.

Ezra smiles crookedly. "A friend once told me it's 'the okayest restaurant in town.'"

I croak a laugh, and some of the tension evaporates. "Sounds about right," I agree. Then I bite my lip, lower my voice. "It's safe to talk here?"

"As safe as anywhere," Ezra says. "I'm not certain if my house is bugged by the MRF."

"And mine?"

He shrugs. "After all of this time? I doubt it."

"But now that I'm back…"

He pauses, and then admits, "I'm the only one who knows you're here."

I blink. "What?"

"I…wasn't sure they'd approve of bringing you in as an, er, consult. This arrangement is off the books."

"So your phone call? Me coming in to see Dorian?"

"All arranged by me and me only." He fidgets. "They know I have a consultant named Gwen. Not your real identity."

I'm not sure if it means I should trust him more or less. "But why? You said the MRF is different now. You don't trust the new management?"

"I trust them to an extent."

It's a lot to process. But at the end of the day, if he's doing this for Dorian's sake, then we're on the same side. "Okay… well. That's good to know." I bite my lip, scrutinizing him. A man willing to lie for the sake of an imprisoned monster. A psychic working at a facility that imprisons and experiments on anomalies like him. "Why are you doing this?" I ask. "What do you want?"

He leans over the table. "I want to help. I've been honest about that from the start."

"At the MRF? We both know their purpose isn't to help."

"Yes, but…" He sighs, pushing hair out of his face. "Before I worked at the MRF, I was studying ghosts. They recruited me based on that work. But before *that,* I was just a kid who always knew he was different."

I know what that's like, but I stay quiet, fingers wrapped around my mug.

"I could feel things that others couldn't," he continues. "*See* things that they couldn't. The first time I met a ghost, it was my grandmother. She came to my bedroom to say goodbye. When my mom told me she was gone the next morning, I said 'I know.' She never looked at me the same after that." His eyes drop to the table before returning to meet mine. "The second time I saw a ghost, it was my best friend. He had been missing for a week. He led me to his body in the creek, and I told the police where to find him. I understood well enough to lie about how I knew at that point.

"When I first got into ghost hunting, I thought I would find others like me. Instead, I realized that I was the only one that could help the spirits I met. I could lay them to rest. I did, for as many of them as I could…and then the MRF found me a few years ago."

Years. I shake my head, pressing my lips into a thin line. "I don't understand how you could work for them." Even if they've changed, they're still the same facility that ripped Dorian away from me and had me locked up in a psychiatric hospital for trying to tell the world the truth.

"I know," he says. "I won't pretend I was ignorant. I knew from the beginning that there was something terrible happening in that building." He grimaces. "I hated what they did to the subjects there. The ghosts trapped in cells, confused and scared, unable to pass on… I can *feel* them in there every day I walk through the halls." Pain and guilt are etched into his features. "I thought if I was there, maybe I could help. I've been doing my best to work under their noses this whole time. I've managed to help some of the ghosts I've worked with pass on. But…" His shoulders slump. "I haven't done enough. Not nearly enough to make up for what I've been complicit in during my time working there.

"But now the facility has changed. And with X-15—with Dorian—I finally have a chance to do something that matters. I thought he was just another spirit I could lay to rest at first. But… I think he might be something different. And he's led me to you." His brows are tilted downward, brown eyes wide, an expression that's almost painfully vulnerable. "I thought I was the only one."

I still don't know if I can trust him, but I do think he's telling me the truth.

Holding his gaze, I reach over and touch the back of his hand.

It's the first time our bare skin has touched since that initial handshake, and again, a strange connection sparks between us. A sense of *kinship*.

Ezra and I each suck in a sharp breath. His eyes shimmer with an odd light for a moment before he blinks it away.

"Wow." He pulls his hand back, stares at his fingers as he flexes them. "Dorian…He's so clear through your eyes. The gloves, the suit…"

I jerk my hand back and clutch it against my pounding heart. "You…saw?"

"Sorry." He pulls his hand back, his excitement fading as he takes in my reaction. "It just happens sometimes."

I swallow hard. After a life of hiding myself from the world, the idea of someone glimpsing my thoughts is *terrifying*. But I'm sure that my abilities frighten people too.

I force a wobbly smile. "That's okay. You just caught me off guard." I cradle my fingers as I study his expression. "You saw him earlier. In the cell."

He nods. "I did. But he was blurry. Not like you can see him."

A strange jolt of relief goes through me. Even though it helps prove once and for all that Dorian is real, for a second, I was almost…jealous. I've always been the only one who could see Dorian. He's always been mine, and mine alone.

The silence stretches out as Ezra and I stare at one another. My fingertips still tingle. Something in me responds to something in him. It makes me want to trust him. It feels like we are *supposed* to help each other. Though maybe that's my superstitious side leaping out again.

"I knew there was something different about you when I met you," he says. "There was…" He gestures. "Like a cloud hanging over you. Initially, I thought it was the connection to Dorian, but it must have just been *you*."

"I felt something the first time I touched you, too." I bite my lip, thinking about everything he's said. Imagining him walking into the MRF every day knowing that he could end up in one of the cells. "You're very brave," I tell him. "I wish I were that brave."

His smile is lopsided, hesitant. "Well, you're here, aren't you? You came back for Dorian."

The only reason I had to come back is because I ran. Because I let myself be convinced that he never existed. But I keep that thought to myself. "So you can see ghosts. And feel things."

He nods. "Emotions. Glimpses of memories, sometimes."

"Can you control it?"

"Not really. It comes in flashes. Can you control yours?"

I huff a laugh. "Did it seem like I decided to fling that table on purpose?"

He laughs as well. "No, I guess not."

"I used to be better at it, I think. But after Dorian… After I left…" I swallow hard. "I bottled it all up. I was desperate to be normal. Now it only comes out when my emotions get the better of me." My *anger*, to be specific, always seems to unleash it. But I don't want to make myself sound dangerous, even if it might be the truth.

Yet as Ezra nods, I wonder how much he already knows, or at least suspects.

"This explains a lot I didn't understand about Dorian," he says. "I suspect your abilities are what allowed him to stay tethered to this plane for so long without passing on. Your influence has likely caused his more…unusual traits, as well." He folds his arms over his chest, looking down. "It also means we have to be careful. If you're anything like me, you're a magnet for spirits. The risk of things going wrong, perhaps even a possession…"

"Dorian would never do that."

Ezra hesitates. "I'm being honest with you, so I need you to be very honest with me." I catch that gleam in his eyes again and wonder if he's reading my emotions. Will he know if I'm lying?

I swallow hard and prepare myself. I know what's coming. "Okay."

"That night you left Ash Valley," he says. "What happened?"

I suck in air, trying to fight the tightness growing in my chest. I dodged this question once; I can't do it again. But I can't bring myself to lie to Ezra, either, even if he's not really reading me. He's right—he's been honest. He's taking a risk for me. It's time for me to tell him the full truth.

"I've seen the report," Ezra continues, when my silence lingers. "The photographs. It's impossible to deny that something terrible happened, but I suspect it wasn't as simple as the MRF wants to believe. I need you to tell me the truth."

The truth. The mere thought of it makes my hands clench in my lap. The words are on the tip of my tongue—they taste bitter, so bitter—but I can't seem to bring myself to say them. A flash of memory: scrubbing blood off my hands, my face, my white dress. Blood everywhere, on the floor and walls and ceiling. An impossible amount of red, red, red.

"Daisy," Ezra says, leaning forward, his eyes intent on me. "Did Dorian kill your parents?"

"I…" I try to force the sentence out, but my throat is so tight, I can barely make a sound. I take in a shaky breath, try again. "Ezra, I…"

He slowly reaches out, takes my hand, and squeezes. "Daisy," he says, even more quietly. "Was it…" He searches my face. "Was it an accident? Did *you* do it?"

I bite my lip as tears well up in my eyes and slowly lift my eyes to meet his. "I don't know."

Surprise flickers across his features. "What do you mean?"

I swallow hard and finally force out the truth. "Ezra, I don't remember. I don't remember that night at all."

Chapter Nine

I pause on the front porch, my hand hovering over the doorknob. Even as a child, I was always averse to inviting people into my home. Because of my parents, and because of Dorian. But also because I was afraid to show them too much of myself.

Yet I'm choosing to trust Ezra. I have to let him in. And it's not as though there are any secrets to find that I haven't revealed to him already. Not any that I remember, at least. So I push the door open and gesture for him to follow me inside.

"Sorry for the cold. It's an old building." I wipe a smudge of dust off a side table. "And I'm still in the process of cleaning it."

"There's nothing to apologize for," Ezra says. "It's beautiful."

I shrug, self-conscious despite his words, and invite him to wait in the living room while I make us a pot of tea. When I head to join him, he's waiting on the couch, hands folded in his lap and eyes on the family portrait that hangs over the mantle. A young version of me stands between my parents. We all look so happy; I wonder if Ezra can see the same strain as I do in my smile.

But when I look at him, his stare is distant, like he's looking through the portrait instead of at it. There's a wrinkle between his brows, and his hands clutch each other in his lap.

"Ezra?" I whisper.

No response.

"Ezra?" I try again, louder, and he jumps and turns to me. His shoulders slump as the tension bleeds out of him, and he shoots me an apologetic smile.

"Sorry," he says. "I thought I felt something. Or heard something. I don't know."

"Something weird?" I ask, my heart rate picking up. "Like…?"

Ezra shuts his eyes, frowning, and slowly shakes his head. "I think it was just you." He opens his eyes again, looking at me. "Your presence can be overwhelming sometimes. Even in the MRF."

I don't know why I asked. Dorian was the only strange thing living in this place, and the only thing it's haunted by now is his absence. I need to get a hold of myself and stop letting the bad dreams get to me.

I set a mug of tea in front of Ezra and sit in an armchair with my fingers curled around my own. Breathing in the smell of chamomile, I let the warmth seep into me. I'm not sure I've stopped shaking since I admitted the truth to him.

"I should've told you right away," I blurt, when I can finally form words. "I… I should've admitted it to the people who came from the MRF that night. But I thought— I was afraid to admit it. And I didn't think they'd be able to capture Dorian. But I was wrong, and so all of these years, I've let him take the blame and the punishment." I blink back a surge of tears. "Dorian never hurt anyone. It probably *was* me."

"Do you remember ever hurting anyone with your powers before that?" Ezra asks. I shake my head. "And have you hurt anyone since?"

"No."

"Then we can't assume it was you, either," he says.

I stare into my tea. He has a point, and I'm not sure if I should be relieved. I don't know what would be harder for me to stomach: the idea that Dorian killed my parents and he's too dangerous to set free, or the idea that I did it and he took the blame these past years.

Either one of us could be a murderer. I don't remember the truth, and Dorian is too scattered to speak of it.

"It isn't just that night missing from my memories," I say. "There are blank spaces. I can *feel* places in my head where things don't make sense. I could be forgetting times where I hurt someone, or Dorian did, or both…" I remember that moment in the observation room where I felt I was on the verge of remembering something. The pain in my skull, the nosebleed… Discomfort shivers through me. Whatever is hidden in my memories, I know it will be difficult to face.

Ezra taps a finger against the rim of his mug. "As far as I see it, there are two possibilities: either we get Dorian to talk to us, or we dredge up your lost memory."

I set my tea aside and lean back in my chair. "I wouldn't know where to begin with solving either of those problems."

"Well…" Ezra tilts his head, thoughtful. "It may just be one problem, actually. It's clear there's a link between the two of you. Whatever is causing your blocked memories may be what has Dorian in such a state as well."

I hug my knees to my chest. "So how can we fix it?" I'm not sure if I mean *Fix him* or *fix me.*

"Well…" Ezra hesitates. Then he seems to shrug off whatever he was about to say. "I suppose we could start with some good old-fashioned detective work."

Chapter Ten

After we part with a promise to meet at the MRF the next day, sleep doesn't come easily. My emotions are a tug-of-war between hope and dread, relief and fear. Ezra is the first person who has ever seen the *real* me since I first ran from Ash Valley. And yet…do *I* even know the real me, with so much of my memory lost?

I bring my laptop to bed and try scouring the internet for anything I can find about my parents, but there's little available. The MRF must have scrubbed everything clean. It's almost as though my parents never existed at all.

My fingers hover over the keyboard. I type: *Dorian Elwood.*

There's not much about him online, either, but I devour the few articles I can find. One has the same picture of a dark-eyed young boy that Ezra showed me. His disappearance was never solved. The details are sparse, but they paint a sad story. A few years before Dorian's disappearance, his mother left the family. And shortly after, Dorian's father killed himself.

One article has a photograph of the three of them. It's blurry and pixelated, but they have the same dark eyes, and they look… troubled. Unhappy. I squint and zoom in further, trying to get a better look at the faces.

Creak.

I freeze at a sound outside of my bedroom, my eyes darting to the open doorway. It almost sounded like a footstep. But try as I might, I hear nothing else.

I shake my head and shut my laptop. No sense in frightening myself with stories like this in a creaky old house. Tomorrow, I hope, Ezra will have answers for us both.

* * *

I'm tense as I walk through the doors of the MRF. Every instinct screams that this is wrong. I'm ready to be apprehended at the gate, at the security checkpoint, in the lobby, but Ezra is the only one waiting for me, smiling as though nothing has changed. As though the truth couldn't get both of us locked up within these walls.

He hands me a coffee, and I manage a small, tired smile. I tossed and turned last night after reading about Dorian, tormented by thoughts of him and imagining I could hear footsteps in the attic.

"Thanks," I say, taking a sip. It's sweet but not too sweet, just how I like it.

"Of course."

Ezra opens the door for me, and I steal a glance at him as I scoot past. I wondered if things might feel different between us now that he knows my secrets. And they do, but not in a bad way. Is this what it's like to have a friend? I've spent so long keeping everyone at arm's length that I hardly remember.

"I took a look at our files before you arrived." Ezra toys with his MRF ID card as he walks. "According to them, it's an open-and-shut case. Dorian killed your parents, they took him into custody, problem solved. But of course, the MRF has historically been in favor of locking monsters up first and asking questions…well, never."

I chew the inside of my cheek. "Right. Was there anything else? Anything useful?"

"They have photographs of the crime scene."

My steps falter. "Oh."

"Yeah," he says. "They're graphic. You're under no obligation to look at them, of course…"

"No," I say. "I-I should. If there's any chance it could help…"

He nods, grim, and reaches over me to scan his ID card and unlock the observation room door. "Go on in, then, and I'll grab those files."

My heart is still racing as I step inside. I pace in front of the observation window, trying to calm my nerves—and nearly jump out of my skin as music starts playing from within the cell.

I step up to the window, pressing my palm to the glass. There's a new radio sitting on the table inside the cell. "Dorian?"

The radio crackles. The song is a familiar one—"Daisy Bell"—but it sounds lower and slower than usual. Sadder.

"I know, Dorian," I whisper. "I'm trying."

The song speeds up again, faster and faster, till it's feverish and panicky. I lean against the glass, wanting, *wanting*—

The door opens, and the radio cuts off. I step back, cheeks flushing, but Ezra's attention is on the folder in his hands.

I join him at the table, and he places it between us.

"Have you seen the photographs before?" he asks.

I shake my head, wordless.

"Like I said, they're graphic," he warns.

My fingers shake as I reach for the file, but I flip it open anyway and look through. It takes every ounce of my willpower not to look away when I see the first photograph of my house's foyer splashed with a torrent of crimson. My mother's twisted body at the bottom of the stairs—all red, raw meat and glint of spine.

Could Dorian have done that? Could I have?

I swallow back bile and flip to the next picture. An axe, its blade coated in blood.

Scraaaape.

I can *hear* the sound, and it makes every hair on my body stand tall.

The axe looks heavy. I'm not sure I could carry it easily. But Dorian? Or...what about my father?

I flip to the next photograph, and that hope extinguishes when I see my father's face cleaved open by that same axe blade. Not just his face—his *skull*, split in half down the middle. He couldn't possibly have done that to himself. The enormous strength it would take...

I imagine Dorian gripping the axe's handle with all four hands, and flinch, dropping the picture.

"Daisy, you don't have to look," Ezra says, mistaking my reaction. He reaches to shut the file as I reach for the next photo, and our fingers accidentally brush. There's a familiar crackle between us, and then Ezra is the one flinching away, color draining from his face.

I go still. "Did you...see something?"

He swallows hard. "Yes," he says. "You were standing at the top of the stairs, looking down at..." He glances at the photographs strewn in front of me and taps the corner of the one depicting my mother's body.

I stare at it, trying to remember what he's describing. But try as I might, I can't.

"You saw something I don't even remember," I murmur, goose bumps rippling over my skin. "How is that possible?"

"The memories are still in there somewhere. You just can't access them."

"What if…you can?" I hold out one of my hands, palm up, in offering.

He stares for a moment before reaching over and clasping my hand. Again, my power sparks from his closeness. But his brow furrows, and he shakes his head.

"I'm not getting anything now. Like I said, it comes and goes."

I blow out a frustrated breath and pull back. I lift my legs onto the chair, wrapping my arms around my knees. "None of this is sparking anything for me, either."

Ezra gathers the papers and shuts the file. "The MRF was eager to blame Dorian and scrub the public record clean to avoid anyone looking into it. I doubt we'll find anything else useful about that night."

I lower my head, my chest tightening as I think of that sad song playing in the cell earlier. "Then…what do we do?" I ask, trying not to give in to despair. "There has to be some way we can help him."

Ezra pauses. "I have an idea, but it might be a little…out there."

I lift my eyes to him. He's hesitating, just like he did last night. Holding something back. "Tell me."

He taps his fingers on the table. "I've spent some time digging through old MRF files. Especially those that are related to psychic abilities. Most of the supposed psychics they brought in were hoaxes." He glances back at the camera, and leans closer to me, lowering his voice. "Still, with a real psychic—with *two* of us—we might be able to apply some of their ideas with more success. But I'm going to need you to trust me."

I've done plenty of reading on the subject too, trying to understand my own nature. MK Ultra, subliminal messages, mind control… Imagining myself locked up in the MRF, electrodes strapped to my head, I hug my knees tighter. I'm not sure I want to know the kinds of things the MRF did to supposed psychics, let alone live through it myself.

But then I remember that glimpse of Dorian through the window. The ache in my chest when I saw his familiar mask for the first time in years. Ezra is right, there is a bond between us, even if I can't remember it. And I *owe* him, my oldest friend.

"I'll do whatever it takes to save him," I say.

Ezra nods. "Have you ever been hypnotized?"

Chapter Eleven

The next morning, Ezra meets me in the MRF lobby again. This time, he holds out a new ID card. "I got permission to take you on as a long-term consultant. This won't give you access to the entire facility, but it will get you through the door without me coming to fetch you every time."

I look down at the card, which has my face and my fake name: *Gwen Bailey*. "Thanks."

I follow him deeper into the facility, into the usual observation room.

My eyes first go to the observation window—showing an empty cell, as usual—and then to the camera in the corner. I quickly look away, but Ezra notices.

"It's all right," he promises, his voice low. "We're just talking. Nothing else. It will hardly be the strangest thing happening within these walls."

I chew the inside of my cheek, unable to fight the fear of someone watching us. What if my powers go haywire again? "But if I say something I shouldn't, or...if I *do* something..."

"I'll handle it," Ezra promises. "Trust me. We should be as

careful as we can, but if the worst happens, I have some favors to cash in."

I nod and turn to the table. An old-fashioned, wooden metronome sits atop it.

"Really?" I ask, shooting Ezra a skeptical look. "Will this actually do anything?"

He shrugs. "It can't hurt."

"I suppose not." I force myself to sit still, folding one leg over the other and placing my hands on the table. "So how does this work?"

Ezra takes a seat across from me. "All you have to do is listen," he says. "I'm going to start by inducing you into a state of heightened suggestion. Your conscious mind will grow quieter and more pliable. Then I'm going to try to walk you back through your memories. You may remember some things without even knowing it, and this could help you bring those memories to the surface."

Fear shivers through me—*maybe I forgot for a reason*—but I quiet the doubt. I need to do this. For Dorian. I glance again toward the viewing panel and the seemingly empty cell beyond.

Ezra follows my look. "He'll be listening to us. As you begin to remember, I hope Dorian will become stronger. Perhaps he'll even be able to communicate with us again." His gaze turns back to me, scrutinizing. "Are you ready?"

I nod again, my mouth dry.

"If you're uncomfortable at any time, say the word and we'll stop."

He turns the key on the metronome, moves the pendulum to the right, and lets it go. It begins to swing back and forth, its beat slow and even.

"Start by watching the pendulum," Ezra says. "Keep your eyes on it as it goes back and forth."

I do as he says, my eyes following its steady movement. *Tick, tick, tick.* I imagine my heart beating in tune.

"Listen to its beat and listen to my voice. If you get lost, let those sounds pull you back to safety. Remember that your body is here, with me, in this room. Nothing you see or hear can hurt you."

Tick, tick, tick.

"Now shut your eyes. Let the sound of the metronome fill your thoughts and everything else fade into the background. Let your breathing slow as your mind empties. One deep breath in…hold it…and let it out."

I breathe with his instructions, and then again, slower than before. The steady ticking of the metronome seems to slow. Ezra's voice, when he speaks again, sounds farther away.

"Breathe in, and let calmness enter… Breathe out, and release your tension. Your body is growing heavier, sinking into the chair. Each breath relaxes you further."

My breathing slows, deepens. My head lolls forward, sinking toward my chest, and rests there. My body seems to fade away.

"Good," Ezra says. "Now we're going to dive into your memories. Imagine them as a void within your mind, filled with sights, sounds, smells…but this void is within you. Right now it is disorganized, floating…but it is all under your control, and you can organize it as you wish."

I imagine myself floating in the darkness, aimless. Peaceful. Fragments of memories floating around me. Dorian's white mask rises from the shadows, his gloved hand stretching toward me. But when I reach for him, he fades.

"Imagine your mind as a house."

I think of my own house. The house I grew up in, with its

many doors. I know every inch of it, every nook and portrait and hidden secret, yet its wide-open spaces are too big for me to fill alone.

"You're standing in the hallway of this house, looking at a series of doors. Do you see them?"

The hallway forms around me. Wooden floorboards stretch beneath my feet, creaking when I shift in surprise; doors rise up on either side of me; the ceiling thumps into place overhead.

"Yes," I whisper to the empty hallway. My voice is loud in the silence. "I'm here."

"Behind each door is a memory." Ezra's voice seems to come from everywhere and nowhere at once, echoing off the walls. "Some of them are locked, but you have the key."

I look down into my hands and see that he's right. I do hold the key, a huge, antique brass thing. I can feel its weight, the faint chill of the metal against my skin, like I just picked it up. I run my thumb over its metal teeth.

"This is *your* house." Ezra's voice sounds fainter, but it's still here with me. "There are no locked doors that you cannot open."

I look down the hallway. There are so many doors, one after another, all wooden and identical and waiting for me. They stretch out endlessly. Every time my eyes wander farther down the hall, more appear.

My breath quickens as my eyes travel further, my chest tightening. "There are so many…"

"It's your decision which ones to open, and when," Ezra says.

His voice pulls me back from the brink of panic. But then my attention snags on the hatch in the ceiling. *The attic.* Just like the first time I saw it in reality, it sends a chill slithering down my spine.

The hatch rattles. I step back. The rattling turns to pounding, like something is throwing itself against the other side.

"I don't want to open the attic," I whisper, struck by a sudden fear that there is something terrible in there. Something better kept locked up.

"You don't have to." I'm grateful for Ezra's voice here with me, calming me down. "It's your house. Your choice. Only you can open the doors, and you don't have to go inside if you don't want to."

I take a deep breath, and another. The rattling slows before stopping entirely. The hallway is quiet; the doors are locked, and I hold the key.

"Ignore the attic," Ezra says. "Whatever is inside will wait for you to be ready. Look at one of the other doors, the closer ones. They hold good memories, ones you want to remember."

I turn to the door on my right. Light spills out from underneath, and I can hear the sound of distant laughter. I recognize it as my own, pitched higher with youth.

"Are you ready to open the door and see?" Ezra asks.

I nod and step forward, sliding the key into the lock. The door creaks open slowly and reveals my childhood bedroom. Identical to now, except without the dust and the cobwebs.

A young version of me sits at my vanity table, carefully arranging my long blonde hair into a ponytail. An invisible hand grabs the end and lifts it, tugging playfully; the younger version of me laughs in delight.

Smiling to myself, I shut it and move to the next door. This version of me is younger still, sprawled across the floor and drawing on a piece of paper with crayons. A pair of eyes watch from underneath the bed while I hum and kick my feet. I step closer, taking a look at the drawing: a small blonde girl, holding hands with a dark figure wearing a mask, slightly larger than she is. The same drawing I showed to Ezra the other day.

"Dorian was always there," I murmur. "He was my best friend. How could I forget…?" Tears prick my eyes, frustration and guilt welling up within me at the thought that I forgot all of this.

The child version of me picks up a black crayon and draws circles around the two figures in the drawing.

"You shouldn't be here," she says in a singsong voice.

I look back at the doorway, expecting to see someone walking in—one of my parents, maybe? But there's no one, and when I turn back to her, she's looking straight at me with an odd smile on her face. She keeps drawing circles while her eyes remain on me. Each movement of the crayon is faster and harder, till I fear it will snap in her tiny hand.

The girl in the drawing is starting to cry, black tears slipping down her cheeks. The masked figure next to her is growing taller and taller. Darkness is all around them.

"Are you talking to me?" I ask. It can't be possible, can it? But…

"You *really* shouldn't be here," she says. Her eyes stay locked on me, her smile is rigor mortis rigid, and a single tear rolls down her cheek.

The lights flicker. When they come back, the drawing is gone; instead, the young version of me holds up a dead magpie.

Somewhere down the hallway, I hear music. Something is pounding on the other side of the attic hatch again.

"Ezra," I say, my voice trembling. "Something's wrong. I want to stop."

"Okay," he says, his voice quiet and muffled, as though through water. "All you have to do is walk back down the hallway—"

The lights go out, leaving me in darkness. My frantic breathing echoes in my ears. A floorboard creaks behind me.

"Ezra, get me out *now*!"

"You're awake," he says, suddenly clear, as if he's speaking directly into my ear. "Open your eyes, Daisy."

I sit up with a gasp. I'm back in the room at the MRF, in a chair at a metal table, a metronome ticking in front of me. Ezra is standing behind me, his hands braced on my shaking shoulders.

"You're all right," he says, and I realize I'm crying. "Daisy, hey. You're here. It was just a memory."

I remember my blank-eyed little-girl stare, the way she *spoke* to me. It didn't seem like a memory. Something felt terribly, terribly wrong. But he's right... Eerie or not, it's not like anything in my own mind could hurt me.

"You went so deep so fast," Ezra continues, sounding almost as shaken as I feel. "It caught me by surprise. It must've been..." He glances toward the camera, turns his back to it, and gestures between us. "One of our abilities, or some combination, I think."

I nod shakily. "Did you see any of what happened?"

"I only heard what you said." He lowers his voice. "But I felt what you felt."

I try to quell my fear. The last thing I need is to give him doubts about our plan. This is the only way for me to get close to Dorian and the truth. I wipe my eyes and force my breathing to steady. The shakes gradually ease.

"I'm sorry," I say, once I have regained some level of composure. "I don't know what came over me. It's just...the *guilt* of it all, the way I left Dorian behind all of these years..."

I look up at Ezra, letting myself be vulnerable. His own expression softens as he looks down at me. "I'm sure this is stirring up a lot of old feelings. It's okay to be emotional about it."

I bite my lip and nod, ignoring the prick of guilt as I swallow my fear.

Chapter Twelve

Step, scrape.

I wake in the middle of the night to a sound outside of my door. A heavy footstep, like a man's boot, followed by a metallic scraping of something being dragged across the floor.

The photograph of the bloodied axe flashes through my mind.

Step, scrape.

Step, scrape.

I clutch my covers to my chest, straining to see in the darkness. My bedroom door is open, moonlight streaming through my window, but there is nothing in the hallway outside. My breath fogs in the air. *Cold, I'm always so cold.*

"Hello?" I whisper.

Step. A floorboard creaks just outside of my door. *Scraaape…*

* * *

I gasp awake to sunlight and blink back confusion and exhaustion. Was that…a nightmare? A memory? I climb out of bed, rubbing my eyes, and pause. There, in the floorboards beside my bed, is an old scuff mark, like something was dragged across it. Something metal. *The axe.*

I swallow hard and reach for a sweater. It's awfully cold in here.

Despite the lingering disquiet, a few hours later I'm back at the MRF, ready to be hypnotized again. I'm not sure what happened yesterday, and I haven't told Ezra what happened last night…but I'm not ready to give up.

I can't deny that I'm terrified of going back into my memories. But I need to remember what happened between me and Dorian. My gut tells me that this is the only way to save him from fading. Ezra seems to think that this is all about a chance for me to say goodbye to Dorian, but I know I can convince him that Dorian belongs with me, if only I can remember enough to prove it.

And like Ezra keeps saying, it's not as though a memory can hurt me. Whatever I find in my own head, it's already happened.

"You sure you're ready to try again?" Ezra asks, looking up from his notebook. "We can give it a few days. Memories may start coming back to you naturally."

I shake my head. "We don't know how much time we have before Dorian fades. I can handle this." I have to be able to handle it.

"Then let's begin."

It's easier this time. It takes hardly any effort on my part. I just let myself be led by Ezra's words, and I'm back in the house of my memories.

It seems even more real than the first time. I can see the dust lining the portraits on the walls, smell the musty scent of a house left empty for too long. The attic access hatch is still there, but it's quiet.

"Remember that you're the one in control here." Ezra's

disembodied voice echoes down the hallway. "This is your mind. These are your memories. Your intent and emotions will guide you through."

I nod, though I know he can't see me here. My intent… I shut my eyes and think. "I want to see a happy memory," I murmur. "I want to see the bond that I've forgotten." Holding that in mind, I move forward with my eyes still shut, stopping in front of a door that feels right, and twist the handle.

When I open my eyes, there is a young version of myself sitting cross-legged on the floor of the attic, reading a book while the record player sings softly in the background. Dorian sits behind me, his chin resting on my shoulder, peering out from behind his mask. He's young, too, slim-shouldered and barely taller than I am. It's strange to see him like this, wearing a T-shirt and jeans, with only two hands instead of four. At a glance, we could almost be two normal children playing together, except for the mask he wears.

With a sudden jolt, I'm living this memory instead of watching it play out. I shut the book and sigh, setting it aside.

"So romantic," I say. "I wish my life could be like that."

"Why shouldn't it be?" Dorian asks—a boyish voice with a whisper of static, coming through the record player while his mouth moves.

"You know why," I say sullenly.

I let out a low whine of protest as he pulls away from my shoulder. But he stands only to bow dramatically and offer a gloved hand to help me up.

I bite my lip. "So dashing," I say, shy all of a sudden.

"I live to serve," he says, eyes crinkled behind the mask.

"Oh yeah?" I grin and shut my eyes, concentrating. When I open them again, his old clothes have shifted into a suit and bowtie, like an old-fashioned butler.

Dorian laughs, delighted, as I take his hand. He lifts me to my feet with ease and places the other hand on my hip. His warmth bleeds through his glove and my skirt, and my stomach swoops.

Dorian leads me in a slow waltz around the room to the sound of the record player. My steps are clumsy, but he is careful and sure-footed as he leads me. When one of my socks slips on a floorboard, I start to fall; he catches me and turns it into a graceful dip.

I giggle, breathless as he lifts me again. I'm as light as a feather in his arms. While plenty of other people make me feel small in a frightening way, with Dorian I know I'm safe.

"Maybe you're right. You are kind of like a real-life prince," I say.

He stops at my words, eyes turning sad. His gloved hand slips free of mine.

"I'm not, though," he says. "I'm more of a monster."

"What?" I clutch him tighter as he tries to pull away from me. "Why would you say that? You're not—"

The thump of angry footsteps drifts up from the hallway below the attic and climbs up the ladder to where we are. Dorian pulls me closer, his eyes narrowing as he glares toward the opening hatch. But even as his shoulders and jaw stiffen, he trembles against me.

"Go," I whisper.

"Daisy…"

"There's nothing you can do. Go," I urge.

Still, he stays. One hand clinging to my shoulder, the other balled into a fist at his side.

When my father reaches the top of the ladder, Dorian steps in front of him. He looks so small in comparison, yet still he stands with his chin up.

But my father steps right through him. He pauses, shivers faintly, and then advances on me.

"What did I tell you about coming up here?" My father's voice is low, dangerous, and slurred.

I hang my head.

"I want to wake up now, Ezra," I say.

"When I snap my fingers, you're back in the room with me," his voice says from somewhere behind me.

My father steps closer, his face like a storm cloud. "And what did I tell you about talking to people who aren't real?"

"Three... two... one..."

My father bends down to grab my discarded book off the floor and rips the cover off. I flinch back, but he grabs my hand before I can retreat.

Dorian yells and swings a fist at him, but it goes through my father's torso. His grip tightens.

Snap.

I blink, and I'm back in my body at the MRF. I lift a hand and wipe away a tear before it can fall. When I lower it again, I study my fingers, the crook in my pinky and ring finger where my father grabbed me in that memory.

"Are you all right?" Ezra asks. "What did you see?"

I drop my eyes to my lap. It's hard to speak about, but I've spent so long keeping it bottled up that I find I *want* to. I need to.

I walk over to the viewing window. Dorian's cell is still empty, but I know he's there.

"I remember now," I say softly, looking through the glass. "I was rarely allowed to leave home when I was a child. Dorian was my only friend."

"What about school?" Ezra asks.

I shake my head. "They insisted on homeschooling me. They said it was because public school wasn't good enough." My lips tilt. They always thought they were too good for Ash Valley, as if they hadn't moved there to escape my father's debts and reputation. "Though mostly, I think it was in case anyone noticed the bruises." I look down at my fingers again, biting my lip. "Dorian was my only escape. The only good thing about life in that house."

I think again of my father's thunderous face in my memory. After seven years, I had almost managed to forget what he looked like, but now it's as bright as a beacon in my mind.

"I know I shouldn't speak ill of the dead, but…" I fold my arms over my chest, hugging myself, remembering how Dorian would hold me like this while I cried. How he'd cry with me, agonized that he couldn't help.

"People should be remembered as they were," Ezra says. "Nothing more and nothing less."

"I agree," I say, my voice quavering as another tear slips free. "So why do I remember so little about Dorian?"

I stare into the cell as if it will give me answers, but they don't appear, and neither does Dorian.

* * *

When I'm standing in the kitchen making tea that night, absently rubbing my crooked pinky again, I suddenly remember a pretend tea party I had with Dorian, his gloved hand holding the porcelain cup so carefully. Pinky out, of course, because we were being fancy.

As I climb the stairs to my bedroom, I remember him walking backward in front of me, showing me where to put my socked feet so the steps wouldn't creak and wake my parents.

The more memories trickle in, the more questions I have. How could I have forgotten all of this? Dorian was my best friend, my only friend. How is it possible I convinced myself, even for a second, that he wasn't real?

Remembering the happy days of our childhood together also makes my day-to-day existence feel even lonelier. I *ache* for Dorian. Sometimes I can barely stand it. I curl up in bed with my hands clutching my stomach, his absence like a physical pain.

And I am still no closer to remembering the most important thing of all: what happened on that fateful night.

Even when I'm in the observation room next to his cell, he feels so far away. It's painful, to be so close but unable to see him or talk to him. This would be so much easier if he were here to talk to me…and it frightens me that he must still be so weak that he cannot. Is he still on the verge of fading? Ezra seems certain that our progress with my memories will help him, but Dorian is so far from what I remember him to be. I never thought of him as something as insubstantial as a *ghost*. In my memories, he was always present and solid and playful.

Yet…he was also shy.

* * *

"Do you think I could talk to him alone today?" I ask the next morning in the observation room.

Ezra hesitates. "I really shouldn't…"

"Just through the glass, I mean," I say. "I'm worried he's hiding because you're here. I've always been the only one who could see him, and…" I don't want to resort to begging, but the tremble in my voice betrays my desperation. "I really just want some sign that any of this is working. How are we supposed to know we're on the right track?"

Ezra shifts his weight from foot to foot, glancing at me and away again. "I can give you five minutes."

I can only stare, stunned into silence. Then I whisper, "Thank you."

I wait until the door shuts behind him and then rush up to the window and press my palm against it, fingers splayed wide. "Dorian," I say through the intercom. "It's me. It's Daisy. Just Daisy. Please, talk to me."

I wait, pulse pounding in anticipation. But nothing happens.

"Dorian, I— I need you to help me. Show me what to do. Show me what I'm missing." I only realize I'm crying when the tears blur my vision. I wipe them away. "Why are you hiding from me?" I ask. "Why can't I remember anything?"

Still nothing. I choke back a sob and step back from the glass.

The moment I do, Dorian flickers into view on the other side. Tall and masked and suited. But his image is faded, blurry, weak in a way that drives a spike of worry through my chest. He presses two of his hands to his heart, as if feeling the same pain. His dark eyes are unreadable.

I gasp and lurch toward the glass, one hand outstretched. As I step forward, he steps back—with a slight delay, a stuttered awkwardness in his movements, like we're separated by time in addition to space.

I stop, fingers slowly curling inward, and lower my hand. The yearning to be with him is like a chain lodged in my chest and pulling me toward him—but I resist it. His aversion is clear, though I don't understand why. I step back, and Dorian moves closer to the window again.

"Why?" I whisper. I keep stepping back; he keeps stepping forward, until he's the one pressed against the glass. "Why are you doing this? Are you angry with me for abandoning you?"

He shakes his head. Again, his movements are jerky, strange.

My lower lip trembles. "Then *why*? All I want is for us to be together again." I don't have to remember everything to know that's true. I feel it deep in my gut, deep in my bones, deep in my heart. We are meant to be together. "Don't you want that too?"

He lowers his head. When he raises it again, his mouth moves behind the slit in his mask, like he's trying to speak—but no sound comes out. A half-second's delay later, a burst of static comes through the intercom.

I shake my head, helpless and frustrated. "I can't hear you."

Dorian leans against the window so that his breath fogs up the glass from the other side. He raises one long, gloved finger and begins to write. One word.

D-A-N-G-E-R.

I glance back at the camera and angle my body so I'm blocking the word from view.

"What danger?" I ask, voice low and urgent. "I'm in danger? You're in danger? Is it the MRF?"

He nods after a moment. I forgot about the delay in his reactions, so it's impossible to tell which question he's answering, and we're almost out of time. Ezra could walk through the door at any second.

"Just tell me what I should do," I plead.

He wipes the word, breathes again, and writes another

message.

R-U-N.

I'm still standing in shock when the door opens and Ezra comes in. My head whips toward him automatically, and I see Dorian disappear out of the corner of my eye. The word—that damning word—lingers on the glass.

But Ezra looks only at me, concern softening his features as he takes in the tears still spilling down my face.

"Did something happen?" he asks. "Did he—"

He starts to turn to the viewing window, but I throw my arms around his neck and pull him into a hug. He freezes before awkwardly patting me on the back. "Daisy… Um…"

I stare over his shoulder at the fogged-up window and cry into his shirt until the letters have faded from view. Then I pull back and wipe my eyes, sniffling.

"Sorry," I say. "This is so hard."

This time, I let him turn to look at the viewing panel. "Still nothing?"

"Still nothing," I lie. "I don't know why he's hiding from me."

Chapter Thirteen

When I next go to the MRF, I find Ezra waiting in the observation room, staring through the window. Dorian's radio is playing a soft, sad song I don't recognize.

I stop beside Ezra. "Anything today?"

"Well, he certainly seems to like the radio. I'm glad I replaced it for him," Ezra says. He turns away, heading to our table and the metronome. "Ready to go again?"

"Yes. I think I'm going to try to find a later memory. Our teenage years, maybe."

Maybe that will help me understand why Dorian is so different now. Why he's refusing to appear to us even though yesterday he proved he can, and why he gave me that ominous warning. Something important must have changed, and the reason must be buried somewhere in my mind.

Ezra nods. "It's your call."

I study him across the table as he sets up the metronome and the recorder. I can't help but wonder if Dorian's warning was about *him*. Does he refuse to appear in front of Ezra because the other psychic poses some kind of threat? Yet I can't quite bring myself to believe it. Everything Ezra has done so far has shown that we're in this together. He's risking his job and his safety for me. In that case, I should probably tell him about Dorian's warning. But I'm afraid he'll shut down our experiments if I do, and I don't think Dorian has time to spare.

I refuse to run away like Dorian wants me to, even if I don't fully understand what kind of danger he's warning me about. I'm not going to leave him again—especially after I saw how weak he was yesterday. I need to find a way to help him, and soon. Right now, my memories are the only lead we have.

"Ready?" Ezra asks, jerking me out of my thoughts.

I nod, folding my trembling hands in my lap. I'm terrified about what I'm going to see as I venture further into my lost memories, but I need to do this.

"Close your eyes and focus on the sound of my voice," Ezra begins, like usual.

It's even easier than last time to follow the sound of the metronome into my memories. The house in my mind appears realer than ever; I can hear the creaks and groans in the old foundation, feel the dust tickling my nose. I hold my intent in mind—*let me see us growing up together*—as I grab a door handle at random. I lift my foot—

My boot comes down with a disorienting *crunch* on gravel. I'm no longer in the house but outside somewhere, on a familiar-but-not street. I barely have a second to reorient myself before a waifish young woman runs past me, long blonde hair streaming behind her. She—*I*—am running hard, chest heaving, face a mask of panic. Moving with the speed of the hunted. And the hunters are not far behind: two teenage boys with their grins full of cruel delight.

"Where you going, Daisy?"

"Crazy Daisy! Crazy Daisy!"

"Come back! We just wanna talk!"

I watch my teenage self stumble past the gate of my house—all fresh white paint in my memory, far from its current dilapidation. I don't have to remember this moment to know it's not going to go the way these boys expect. I smile as I follow them into the front yard of my home.

Teenage me collapses just past the front gate, breathing hard. She licks her split lip; I taste blood. But as she rests her palms on the gravel around her, I know she's no longer afraid. The boys are no longer the hunters here, but they don't realize it as they skid to a stop a couple of feet from her.

"Running home to Mommy and Daddy?" one of them asks, his voice mocking. "You think they're going to rescue you?"

I shake my head half a second before the teenage version of me does. "Not them," I say.

The boy sneers. "Who else would care enough to help you?"

We both pause, heads tilting. Waiting, and then smiling. "Him."

A gloved hand shoots up from the ground and grabs one of the boys by the ankle. It yanks, and the boy falls on his face with a yelp of shock and pain. "What the f—" is all he has time to say before he's yanked backward, hands scrabbling for purchase on the gravel.

We watch him, a ghost of a smile still on our lips.

The other boy blanches. He takes one step back, and another, watching his friend be dragged out the front gate. "Please don't hurt me," he says.

I look at the gravel embedded in my palms from the fall. "*I'm not doing anything*," I say, and smile as a gloved hand taps on his shoulder. He whirls around and goes white as a sheet as he comes face-to-face with…nothing, as far as he can see.

But I see a white mask, and two gloved hands that shove the boy backward.

Dorian and I both watch as the boy runs screaming from the property. Then he bends down and offers me a gloved hand, the perfect gentleman. I take it and grin as he lifts me up. When he sets me on my feet, my head barely reaches his shoulder.

Teenage Dorian is long and lanky, his dark hair worn shaggy. Messy strands fall in front of his white mask as he tilts his head down to meet my eyes.

"My protector," I say, and stand on my tiptoes, tugging on the front of his shirt. He obligingly leans down so I can plant a kiss on the cheek of his mask—but at the last second, he turns his head.

My lips touch only cold porcelain, but I can feel his breath through the mouth hole of his mask, so very close. Mischief lights his dark eyes.

"You—" I sputter, flushing red but grinning. I reach for his hand and—

The world spins around me as the memory changes.

I'm still standing on the edge of the property. But now I'm pulling at Dorian's hand desperately, tears streaming down my face. He's even taller than the last memory, his shoulders broader and stronger, and he's grown an additional set of hands, each one gloved. I grasp at one hand with both of mine while the other three hang limp at his sides.

"Come with me," I beg. "There has to be a way!"

Dorian's feet are stopped just beyond the gate, and his gloved hand is stuck midair in the same spot, like it meets an invisible barrier there. No matter how hard I strain, I can't get him to move.

His eyes are sad behind the mask. He shakes his head.

"I can't leave without you," I sob, frantic. "I can't go on my own…"

"Daisy!"

* * *

I startle awake, head spinning. I'm back in the room at the MRF. Ezra has me by both arms and is shaking me as he shouts my name. My head lolls to the side, and I swear I see Dorian at the viewing panel. But when I turn that way, he's gone again.

"I'm— I— What happened?" I ask, disoriented.

Ezra's shoulders slump in relief as he lets me go. "Oh, thank God," he says. "I've been trying to wake you up for five minutes. You went completely unresponsive." He grabs a tissue and holds it out to me. I stare for a moment before I feel the trickle of blood from my nose and take the tissue to dab at it. As I do, I notice that my palms are bleeding too, scraped raw and pockmarked. I must've been gripping the edge of the table.

"That hasn't happened before?" I ask him.

He shakes his head. "You usually talk to me while it's happening. But this time you were completely gone."

"It felt different," I murmur, pressing the tissue against my nose. I almost forgot it was a memory; it was disorienting to jolt back to the present.

And Dorian was different in that memory, too. When we were children, he couldn't touch my father. But as a teen, he was able to physically drive off those boys. He was so much stronger…yet still trapped on the grounds.

And I was trapped, too. With him and my parents. What a

horrible irony that the MRF found a way to free Dorian, only to trap him here instead.

If not for the MRF, we could've lived together so happily once my parents were dead…

I jolt out of my thoughts. Ezra is still staring at me, brow furrowed with concern.

"If this is dangerous for you…" he says.

I shake my head. "It doesn't seem dangerous," I lie. "I feel like I'm moving forward. Like I'm starting to remember things." I wipe my nose one last time, see no spots of new blood, and toss the dirty tissue into the wastebasket. "Did Dorian react?"

"I didn't see him, but the EMF reading was going haywire, and the radio started playing a song."

"Was it 'Daisy Bell'?"

Ezra shakes his head. "No. 'Run, Rabbit, Run!'"

"Hm." I shrug. "Well… Those are good signs, right?"

Ezra huffs a strained laugh. "I don't know anymore."

"But it means Dorian's getting stronger!"

Ezra still looks hesitant but nods. "I guess so." He returns to his side of the table and sits down, flipping his notebook open. "Now, describe what you saw."

As I give him a censored version of the memory—leaving out the fact that Dorian could physically harm people—I stare down at the dried blood on my tissue and return to that guilty thought again and again.

We could've been so happy together, once my parents were dead.

Chapter Fourteen

Days pass, and then weeks. Ezra continues to lead me through the endless hall of memories inside of my mind. I remember more of Dorian, both inside of the MRF and outside of it. I begin to put together the puzzle pieces of our past.

The more I remember about our friendship and his protectiveness over me, the lonelier I am every night I climb into bed alone. I stay awake, listening to the creaks and groans of the house and wishing he were here. Sometimes I think I hear the sound of music as I'm drifting to sleep. Sometimes it's footsteps pacing up and down the hall, or the scrape of something metal dragging against the floorboards. Nightmares plague my sleep, but every time I wake up sweating and gasping, I can't remember what I dreamed about.

Dorian's presence in the cell is fleeting, evanescent. Occasionally, he plays a song on the radio, usually "Daisy Bell," or sometimes flickers through stations. I always strain to hear a whisper of his voice or some hidden message, but I can't.

Once or twice, I catch a glimpse of him through the window, always out of the corner of my eyes, and he's gone when I turn my head.

Ezra assures me it's good news, that the EMF spikes and the temperature drops whenever I'm present and talking. But Dorian is nowhere near as strong as he was in my memories. All I can do is press forward, hoping that something hidden in my mind will help me figure out *why*.

Yet I still haven't found the courage to open that hatch to the attic in my mind, the one that frightens me so badly. And I can't stop thinking about Dorian's one clear message to me: his warning to *run*.

There must be more to the story that I haven't remembered yet. The answer must be somewhere in my memories. And I know that eventually I'm going to have to open that hatch.

The next time I'm in the MRF, I'm still not brave enough to do it. But when I reach for the next door to a memory, that fear lingers in my mind. It curls around my heart as I turn the knob, and—

* * *

In this memory, I'm in my late teens, treating myself to a mini spa day, using the clawfoot porcelain tub in my bathroom, the room lit only by candles. I hum to myself as I stretch out in the warm water, lavender-scented bubbles covering me from the neck down.

When the door creaks open, it doesn't frighten me. I open my eyes just long enough to see that there's nobody standing there and then shut them again. "I'm in the bath, Dorian."

Footsteps pad toward the tub. Heat rushes to my face, and I sink lower into the bubbles to hide myself. I'm still embarrassed at the thought of him seeing me naked like this, even though it wouldn't exactly be the first time.

"*Dorian*," I chide, but I'm smiling despite it. It's still *new*, this thing between us, but… I'm eighteen now, and my parents are gone for the weekend, so maybe it's finally time.

Self-consciousness melts away as he pushes my wet hair to the side and caresses my neck, sending shivers through my body despite the warm water. When cool hands run down over my shoulders, massaging the muscles there, I lean into his touch.

I sigh, leaning my head back against the side of the tub. "That feels nice." The grip on my shoulders tightens. Thumbs dig into my skin hard enough to make me wince. "Less nice."

The fingers dig in harder. Bruising. My eyes fly open just as the candles in the room flicker out at once, dousing the room in darkness. The steam in the air is suddenly thick, choking. A coppery stink floods my nose, my throat. The water becomes viscous and sticky against my skin, and when I look down, I gasp. The tub is filled to the brim with blood. "Wait, this isn't—"

The hands shove me under the surface. I scream out a stream of bubbles, fighting and thrashing to no avail. I claw at the hands holding me, but their grip only tightens. Hard as steel, impossibly strong. I try to cry out and choke on a mouthful of coppery liquid. It rushes into my nose, my throat, my lungs—

* * *

I cough out a mouthful of liquid and gasp for air. When my eyes flutter open, I'm no longer in the bathroom. I'm in the MRF, on the floor, with Ezra leaning over me. Static is blaring through the intercom from Dorian's cell, the lights flickering. My eyes roll toward the observation window, and Dorian is there, all four hands pressed to the window and his eyes locked on me.

When our gazes meet, I find the faintest flicker of relief in his eyes before he disappears. The static cuts off and the lights steady.

I turn over and choke up another mouthful of liquid. It's only water, thank God—but then a drip of blood falls, tinging it pink. I wipe at my face; my nose is bleeding again.

"What—" I'm shivering, struggling to get the words out through chattering teeth. "What happened?"

Ezra thumps a hand against my back, making sure the water is done coming up. "I-I don't know," he says. "You went catatonic on me again. And then you started—" He shakes his head. His hands tremble where he holds me. "Just, choking. Drowning. On nothing but air. I thought you were—" He cuts off as his voice breaks.

I cling to him. "It's okay. I'm okay."

"Are you?" He searches my face. "What was that? What happened? Was it a *memory* that did that?"

I stare up at him. "I don't know," I whisper. "Is that possible?" But I know, even as I ask it, that he doesn't have any more answers than I do.

This whole time, we've been operating under the assumptions that my memories can't actually hurt me, but today might have shown us how very wrong we were.

"What happened in the memory?" Ezra asks. "I heard you say Dorian's name. Did he…hurt you?"

"No," I say quickly.

Too quickly.

Ezra pulls away, his expression guarded. "Daisy, I'm trying to help you, but you have to be honest with me."

"I *am* being honest," I insist, even as I wonder if it's the truth.

"It wasn't him. I'm not sure it was even a real memory. Maybe it started as one, but then something… I don't know, something went wrong. It's like my memories are tainted. I don't know what's real and what's not." I run shaky fingers through my hair. My body is dry, but I'm freezing like I was plunged into water.

Ezra shrugs off his blazer and drapes it over my shoulders. When his fingers nearly brush mine, I flinch back.

He pauses. "I want to help Dorian too," he says. "But not if it's going to get you hurt. If Dorian is dangerous, I need to know so we can progress safely."

"He isn't dangerous!" Not to me, at least. I'm *sure* of that, regardless of that memory.

"Even if that's true, your memories clearly are," he says. "If they can hurt you like they did today, what's going to happen to you if you go back to that night?"

I think of that locked attic hatch in the hallway of my memories. The way it shook. My bone-deep terror at the thought of opening it.

Ezra's expression mirrors my own fear. "We can't keep doing this," he says. He takes a deep breath, blows it out, and walks to the observation desk.

"But I saw him," I say hoarsely. "It's working."

Ezra looks at the readings on his devices and sighs. "It is," he admits. "The temperature plummeted and the EMF showed the strongest reading yet." He looks at me. "But that means Dorian is stronger than ever. He'll be fine if we take a break."

Still shivering, throat raw from choking up water, I can't bring myself to argue.

* * *

I spend most of my two days off sleeping, yet I stumble into the MRF again feeling like I've barely slept at all.

When I step into the observation room, the radio sputters to life in Dorian's cell—playing "Run, Rabbit, Run!"—and my nose immediately spurts blood. I swoon on the spot.

Ezra catches me before I hit the floor and sends me home again, which is both a frustration and a relief. He promises to do more research into hypnosis and scour the MRF files for anything useful. He sounds doubtful, though, and I feel the same. We're the only psychics who have tried this, to our knowledge. It's new territory.

As eager as I am to reunite with Dorian, I have to admit it's a relief not to venture back into my memories for a little while.

But stuck at home, the days crawl past. Now that I've uncovered some of the holes in my memory, it's like a constant, nagging itch in the back of my consciousness. Without hypnosis to rely on, I return to the old-fashioned way of snooping around my childhood home. I rummage through my bedroom in the hope that I'll find something that will spark a memory.

Most of what I find is mundane. A hairbrush makes me recall how Dorian would tug on the end of my braid to tease me when we were children. A pearl necklace has me smiling as I remember him helping me clasp it around the back of my neck, his invisible fingers brushing my skin. God, I miss him.

It couldn't have been him pushing me under the water in that memory. I refuse to accept it.

When the ache in my chest becomes too much to bear, I crawl under my bed and lie there on the floorboards. This was the first place I saw Dorian, and I remember hiding here with him when he was too frightened to come out. I trace my fingertips over the letters of my name carved into the bedpost.

Then I notice a piece of paper crumpled between the mattress and the bedsprings. I tug it free and smooth it out. I expect to find one of the pictures I loved to draw when I was a kid, but instead it's a list, written in black crayon in my own childish handwriting.

The rules

1. *Don't look at him*
2. *Don't say his name*
3. *Don't think about him!*

My brow furrows as I mouth the words. What was this? Some kind of game? Yet it feels important, since I tucked it away here, beneath my mattress, like some kind of secret treasure.

A floorboard creaks in the hallway outside my room.

My head whips in that direction and my heart skips a beat. I hold my breath, listening. Was that a footstep? It sure sounded like it, but the house is quiet now.

Don't look.

I can almost hear the words, like they're being whispered right in my ear. In a flash, I remember hiding under the bed, peering out at the doorway just like I am right now. My hands clenched and my heart pounding. *Don't look don't look don't look—*

A blink. A drip. And I'm back in the present, blood trickling from my nose. I sigh and crawl out from under the bed, reaching for a tissue. These nosebleeds are such a pain. It felt like I was on the verge of remembering something important, but now my concentration is broken and the moment is gone.

Still, as I staunch the bleeding, my eyes keep drifting back to the doorway, and I keep somehow expecting to see someone, or something, there, watching me.

* * *

My ringtone jolts me awake in the middle of the night. I fumble for my phone on the nightstand, squint at Ezra's name, and hastily answer.

"What happened?" I ask. My heartbeat is already rising. A weekend phone call in the middle of the night can't be good news.

"It's Dorian," Ezra says. "I was concerned about how little activity I've seen over the past couple of days, so I came in today to check on him, and…" His breath hitches. "I'm not seeing any sign of him. Nothing's registering on the EMF, the temperature sensor—nothing."

I'm already scrambling out of bed. "I'm on my way."

"Daisy." His voice is gentle in a way that threatens to tear me apart. "It might be too late already. I don't know—"

I hang up before he can finish the sentence. *No.* I can't let myself believe it's over. Not when we finally seemed to be making progress. Not when I'm so close to figuring out the truth. Not when I haven't even had a chance to say goodbye.

I throw a coat over my nightgown and race out to my car, oblivious to the chill in the air. The streets of Ash Valley are dark and empty at this time of night, so there's nothing to slow me down as I race to the MRF. But once I reach the gate, I'm forced to stop. Of course, there's still a guard on duty, and he peers at me with obvious suspicion. I clench the wheel, trying to calm myself down before I say or do something stupid. Power sizzles beneath my skin, searching for an escape. To let it out here and now would be an abysmal mistake.

"I-I forgot my ID, but I'm here to assist Ezra Bradford," I tell the guard. "It's an emergency."

"He didn't say anything about—"

"Call him," I snap. The guard's brow furrows, and I realize that the wheel is vibrating under my hands, the car radio flickering through different stations. I remember how important it is to contain my anger. I shut my eyes, breathe, and push the overflow of energy down, deep down. "Please," I say, when I'm sure I can keep my voice steady.

The man turns away from me and grabs his radio. His words are too quiet for me to overhear. I watch through the window, well aware how easy it would be for Ezra to have me turned away. But the guard waves me through the gate.

I park and then race into the building, pulling my coat tighter around me as the winter night bites at my bare legs. Ezra's in the lobby when I arrive, holding out his hands as if to placate me.

"Let me see him," I demand.

"Daisy, I told you…"

"I know what you told me." My voice trembles despite my best efforts to stay calm. Now that I'm here, seeing the sorrow on Ezra's face, reality is threatening to crash down on me. "I'm not going to believe it until I see it for myself. I *need* to see. To try. To…to say goodbye, if nothing else." I try to blink back my tears, but they overflow anyway, trekking down my face. "Please, Ezra."

Ezra scrubs a hand across his face. "You can try to talk to him," he says. "Maybe he'll hear you, if it's not too late…" The doubt in his voice is obvious, but I can tell that he wants this to work almost as badly as I do.

We both hurry down the hallway to the observation chamber. Once inside, I rush to the window and press both hands against the glass. The intercom is already active; Ezra must have been trying to speak to Dorian before I arrived.

"It's me," I say. "Can you hear me? Please, show me that you're still there."

But there's no movement in the room, no noise. The radio sits silent. The cell stays empty. I shut my eyes and try to reach out, to *feel* some hint of his presence, but there's nothing but an empty room.

"No," I whisper.

Ezra stands behind me. A beep draws my attention, and I turn to see the EMF reader in his hands, sitting at a steady green. *No activity.*

We both stare at the meter, waiting, but there's no change.

My hope is withering. Ezra is sensitive to spirits, and I am sensitive to Dorian. I trust both of us more than any device, but if neither of us can sense him anymore...

"But it was working," I say, my voice thick with tears. "You said he was getting stronger."

"He *was*," Ezra says, his shoulders slumping. "Hearing his name, his memories, seeing you...that's how ghosts get stronger. I'm certain it helped. But maybe it was a temporary burst of strength. Maybe he held on just a little longer for a chance to say goodbye to you."

I press a hand to my mouth, choke back a sob. "But I didn't get to say goodbye," I say. "You didn't let me see him. If you had just let me in..."

Ezra stares at the floor, emotions warring on his face. "I had to protect you, too," he says.

Fury wells up inside, filling the empty ache in my chest. It is easier to have someone to blame, and Ezra is right in front of me.

"You were protecting *yourself*," I snap. "And your job."

The pity in his face only makes me angrier. "All ghosts pass on eventually, Daisy. It's what they do. They're just echoes of the past. I was hoping to offer Dorian a chance to speak with you and resolve things before that happened, to give *you* a chance at closure, but it was always going to go this way eventually. He's at peace now."

I shake my head, furious tears spilling over. "No," I whisper. "No, Dorian is different. He wasn't supposed to go."

I shut my eyes. I'm furious with Ezra, but also at myself. For my cowardice, my refusal to face the hard memories that might've told me something valuable about my history with Dorian. Instead, he's gone before I had a chance to find the truth.

"It's not your fault," Ezra says. I'm not sure if he's reading my emotions or if they're written all over my face. "We did our best."

He reaches for me, but I pull away. I don't want to be comforted. If this terrible emptiness—this all-consuming grief—is what I have left of Dorian, then I hope I feel it every day of my life.

"I want to say goodbye," I say.

Ezra nods, looking away. "I can leave the room and let you…"

"Not here." I press my hand to the glass. "In there. If I can't see him again for a real goodbye, at least let me be where he was. Maybe I can…" My voice trembles again, and I stop, swallowing hard. "Maybe there's some hint of his presence left behind."

Ezra looks between my face and the empty cell. He's silent for a long moment. And then, finally, he nods. "Okay," he says.

"I can… I'll cover the camera. Give you a few minutes. That's all I can do without someone getting suspicious."

It's not much. Barely anything at all, really. But I know he's already taking a risk, so I don't dare ask for more.

* * *

A few minutes later, Ezra leads me into the cell where Dorian was. All this time it's been just on the other side of the glass, so close yet so out of reach, locked behind two iron doors to keep him from escaping. Now, Ezra shuts the door behind me, and I'm alone in the space that Dorian used to occupy.

This place is terrifyingly reminiscent of the time I spent institutionalized. When I think of being strapped down in bed, drugs turning my thoughts to sludge, it feels like the walls are closing in on me. But the fear oozes away as quickly as it hit me. I thought that was the worst thing that could happen to me, but this proves me wrong. The true horror is a life without Dorian in it.

I stand in the center of the room and look around, wishing I could feel anything other than a hollow ache my chest. I look at the cot set up in the corner, the table with the radio sitting on top. White walls, white floor. The viewing panel is shuttered from the other side to grant me privacy, making the room nothing more than a closed box. For years, Dorian was trapped in this room. Alone. Abandoned by me when I fled Ash Valley.

And now, just when I've come back for him, he's gone.

Something inside of me crumbles. I fall to my knees on the floor, a cry ripping out of my throat. When it breaks through the numbness, the sadness is unimaginable. Like a physical blow to the stomach. I'm drowning in the loss, like I will never feel anything other than grief ever again.

But not just grief. *Anger.* Anger that Dorian was torn from me in the first place, that he was trapped here for years without me knowing how to reach him. Anger at myself for not being able to conquer my memories for his sake. Anger at the unfairness of it all.

I scream into my hands, letting out everything I've been bottling up for so many years. The room trembles around me; the table and the bed shake, only remaining grounded because they're secured to the floor. The radio lifts off the table, floating. The air pulses, brimming with overflowing energy. I have so much anger and no way to let it out.

I wonder if I could bring this building crumbling down. If I could tear apart the walls that kept me separated from Dorian until it was too late. It might be worth it, even if I bury myself in the wreckage…

A hand grasps my shoulder.

A gentle squeeze coaxing me back from the brink. Dragging me up from the whirlpool of my emotions. The room stops shaking; the radio clatters to the table. I tilt my head back and look up into a blank white mask.

My heart stops. For a moment, I can only gape. And then I say, voice trembling, "Dorian?"

Chapter Fifteen

As he reaches to cup my cheek, Dorian's glove is warm and leathery and familiar against my skin. I shut my eyes, breath hitching, hardly able to believe this is real. But when I open my eyes again, he is still standing there. More solid than his earlier appearances, barely a blur around his edges. My gaze combs over him—the dark eyes behind his white mask, all four gloved hands hanging at his sides, that all too familiar suit that I always found so dashing.

Perhaps I should be afraid. The mystery of my parents' murders…that recollection of almost drowning in the bathtub…the way he's changed over the years since I abandoned him. All of those things seemed so important before tonight, when I faced the reality of losing him.

Now, I clamber to my feet and throw my arms around him. *"Dorian. But how…?"*

He tries to pull away from me, but I clutch him closer—needy, desperate to know that he's solid and real and *here*. And after a brief hesitation, all four arms wrap around me and his chin settles on my head.

As Dorian holds me for the first time in years, I find that I don't care enough about the *how*. I hadn't realized how cold I was, shivering on the tile in my nightgown and my coat, until his warmth surrounded me. I have never felt as safe as I do now. My body knows him even if I can't remember the details.

"You're here," I whisper. I stand on my tiptoes to press my face into his chest, wind my fingers into his dark hair, hold him as tightly as I can. I will hold him forever if it means he will stay visible and solid and real. I want to climb under his skin, stitch us together so we can never be separated again. "Don't disappear on me again. Please. *Stay.*"

Before I'm aware of what I'm doing, I reach up and pull his face toward me. He yields to my touch, and I push his mask just above his mouth and kiss him.

When our lips collide, I know that it's *right.* The contact sends a shock all the way through my body, tingling in my fingers…and elsewhere. Dorian's grip on me tightens, all four hands clutching at me like he wants to somehow pull me closer. He kisses me back with hunger to match mine. Hot breath, a slide of tongue. A whimper escapes me as he crushes me against his chest, my breasts rubbing against his stomach; even through his suit, I can feel the hard muscles of his abs. I kiss him again and again, until I am panting, and even then it is not enough. I nip his bottom lip, breathe him in; I'm struck by a desire to consume him. To be consumed.

I have always kept everyone else at arm's length, but Dorian can never be close enough. I need him. I've always needed him. How could I have forgotten *this*?

He pulls away, breath shuddering out. I catch a glimpse of full, swollen lips, and then he yanks his mask down to cover his mouth again.

"Daisy," he whispers.

I freeze at the sound of his voice coming from the radio.

Deep and whispery and all too familiar. He still sounds far away, distorted, like a channel with a bad connection. But he *spoke*.

I gaze up at him in wonder. "Dorian."

"Can't be…" His mouth keeps moving, but the words turn to static. "D-D-D—"

My heart wrenches. "I can't hear you."

He reaches up to wipe my face. When he draws his hands back, his white glove is red and wet with blood. I wipe at my nose; I hadn't even realized it was bleeding. He clenches his hand into a fist.

"It's okay," I tell him. "It's just from using my powers, I think." I wipe my nose again; it won't stop bleeding. "I'm fine."

He shakes his head.

"Danger!"

I flinch at the burst of noise from the radio, clasp a hand to my ear as it crescendos in an awful shriek of sound before cutting off. When I look back at Dorian, he's going fuzzy around the edges again. Fading.

"Don't go," I plead. I reach for his shirt, but my hand goes through him. "Tell me what's going on!"

The door to the cell opens. "Daisy? I just saw something on the EMF, are you…?"

I look over my shoulder at Ezra, who freezes in the doorway, staring. Then back toward Dorian, expecting him to have disappeared already—but he hasn't. He's still standing there, his masked face tilted to one side as he looks at Ezra. His eyes narrow, his shoulders stiffening.

Then two of his gloved hands jut out and *shove* me backward. Gasping, I stumble directly into Ezra, sending us both falling to the tile. While we're still sitting there, Dorian grabs the door and shuts it behind him, closing himself in his cell.

* * *

I stand in front of the viewing window, holding a tissue to my nose and watching Dorian walk around the room. After the fleeting appearances of the last few weeks, followed by what seemed to be a total disappearance, it's shocking to see him so clearly. He is so visible and...*real*. He doesn't so much as flicker as he paces the room, and when he pauses to pick up the rubber ball and bounce it against the floor, it's obvious that he is still solid as well.

"You can still see him?" Ezra asks.

I smile without taking my eyes off Dorian. "Yes."

Beside me, Ezra fusses over an array of instruments on the desk—the EMF reader, a temperature gauge, and more that I don't understand. As he records numbers in his notebooks, his eyebrows lift toward his hairline. "Amazing," he murmurs. "Dorian hasn't shown such a solid manifestation in the entire time I've been observing him." He looks up from his notebook at me with something like awe. "You brought him back. He was *gone*, and you brought him back."

I drop my gaze. "I don't think I did anything special."

"Regardless, the strength of your bond is impressive." He shuts his notebook and comes to stand beside me, peering through the viewing window.

"Can you see him now?" I ask.

"Mm...sort of. If I concentrate. I can definitely *feel* him now, like I can with other spirits."

Dorian pauses as he notices Ezra in the window, and stiffens.

Then he disappears from view. The ball drops from his hand and bounces against the floor before rolling to a stop.

I hit the intercom. "You don't have to be shy. Ezra is helping you. Helping *us*."

The coloring book and crayons fly off the table and hit the wall. A burst of static comes through the radio, and the lights flicker.

"Be nice," I scold. "Ezra is my friend."

The coloring book flips over, and a crayon scribbles: *MINE MINE MINE.*

"I'm allowed to have other friends," I say.

The crayon snaps in half and clatters to the floor.

I flinch at the crack of it, my mind leaping to that last hypnosis session, the memory of being pushed down in the tub by invisible hands.

But that memory was *wrong*. Dorian would never do that to me.

I clear my throat, turning to Ezra. "I'm sorry."

His lips lift in a half-smile. He's looking into the cell, distracted enough to miss my doubt. "I'm just happy to see that he's strong enough to act out like this." He folds his arms over his chest, drumming his fingers against the opposite bicep. "Though I hope we can find a way to get him to cooperate."

My good mood dampens. He's right. Bringing Dorian back from the brink of nonexistence was only the first step in us being reunited.

"Can't you let me bring him home?" I ask, my voice barely more than a whisper. "You...you could tell the MRF he disappeared today and let me leave with him. Couldn't you?"

Ezra opens his mouth, shuts it again. When he finally speaks, instead of an answer, he asks, "Why did he push you out of the cell?"

I blink. "What?"

"I saw him push you," he says, studying my face. "Like he didn't *want* you to be there. Why?"

"I…" My mouth hangs open before I shut it and wordlessly shake my head.

"Have you remembered what happened that night?" he presses. "Do you know if he killed your parents?"

I flush under his scrutiny and lower my eyes. I believe, deep in my heart, that Dorian didn't do it…but he's right that I don't know for certain.

"There are too many things we don't know," Ezra says when I don't respond. "I've always suspected there was more to the story of what happened that night, but Dorian still isn't communicating with us. He seems unstable. And like I said before, sometimes, spirits can warp. Lose themselves. I need to be sure that isn't happening, and Dorian is harmless to you and the rest of the world, before I can think about doing something like that."

I almost insist he is, but I stop short. I *am* certain Dorian is harmless to me. But the rest of the world?

"And if I *can* prove that?" I ask, lifting my eyes to meet his again. "Then what? Will you help me get him out of here?"

"Yes," he says without hesitation. "If we do this right…" He turns and looks at Dorian's cell, a fragile hope blooming on his face. "I've told you the MRF is different now. The new leadership is sympathetic. If we could prove that he's harmless, maybe they'll agree to release him."

I stare at him, searching his face. I've been nursing a vague hope that Ezra would help stage an escape for Dorian if I could convince him he was innocent, but I never dared to dream of *that.* "You think that's possible?" I ask. "This place, you think they would actually let him go?"

"I do," Ezra says. "And I think it could change everything about the MRF's future."

I bite the inside of my cheek, nodding. It's hard to make myself care about the MRF. But it means my interests and Ezra's are aligned, for now.

"So where should we start?" I ask, gazing into the cell.

Dorian reappears, grabbing his rubber ball from the floor and beginning to toss it and catch it again, alternating between his four arms.

I can still feel those arms around me. All four hands touching, caressing, grabbing, like he can't get enough.

Ezra squints through the viewing window, his brow furrowing. "Does he…? His arms. It almost looks like…"

"He has four of them," I say, smiling. But Ezra's startled look makes my grin fade. Surely that can't be the most unusual thing Ezra has heard of in this place.

"But that's…" He shakes his head, pushes his glasses up. "In the drawing you showed me, he only had two."

"Yeah, he grew them later," I say.

"When?"

"I…" I'm about to say "I don't remember" when a memory jolts through my brain. *I'm pinning Dorian down in bed, grinning in triumph as I hold his wrists at his sides. But his eyes turn sly behind the mask, and suddenly two more hands sprout from his torso and grab me. He twists so he's on top and leans down to—*

I blink away the memory, heat rising to my face. A trickle of wetness at my nose alerts me to more bleeding, and I wipe at it hastily before Ezra can see. "I-I… Is that important?"

"I suppose not," Ezra says, staring at Dorian instead of me.

"I'm just trying to understand." He glances down at his notebook and shakes his head. "But you're right. We should focus. He's here now, so maybe he can answer our questions?"

"Right," I say quietly. Did my contact with Dorian crack the dam holding back my memories? Something to explore later, but for now, Ezra is right. I can just *ask* Dorian about that night instead of trying to drag the truth from my fractured mind. I should've suggested it myself…or maybe some part of me was—is—afraid of what his answer might be.

But I have to ask. I have to know. I suppress my nerves as I reach over to press the intercom button. "Dorian?"

Dorian flickers out of existence. The rubber ball drops to the floor, bounces a couple of times, and stops. Then all of a sudden he is back, standing just in front of the viewing window, his head tilted to one side and his mask practically pressed against the glass.

"Can I ask you a question?"

He spreads his gloved arms, hands out, as if to say "Be my guest."

Now that the opportunity to ask him has finally arrived, my mouth is dry. Dorian spoke to me when I was in the cell—maybe he will again. This is an opportunity to face the truth… But am I going to like what I find out? I'm all too aware of Ezra listening and taking notes beside me.

I swallow hard, and my voice shakes as I ask, "Could you tell me about what happened? The night…the night my parents died?"

Dorian is still and silent on the other side of the glass. Then his neck twitches and he steps back, clasping both sets of hands behind his back. It's impossible to read his emotions behind that smiling mask.

The radio on the table flickers to life and begins to flicker through stations.

An official-sounding broadcast: "This is an emergency alert." A crackle of the station changing, now a singer crooning sadly. "Oh, my darling—" Crackle, shift to an upbeat advertisement. "—running out of time! Act now or—" Crackle. "Hello darkness…"

My brow furrows as the radio fades into static. "I don't understand," I whisper. "I'm running out of time to…save you? I know that. That's why I'm here."

Dorian shakes his head. I can sense his frustration mirroring my own. Once, it was so easy for us to understand each other, but now there's a gap that feels impossible to overcome.

As I'm trying to think of other ways to communicate with him, the radio buzzes to life again. A familiar, jaunty tune. "Run, Rabbit, Run!" starts to play. I glance toward it, an odd prickling sensation spreading across my skin as my memory strains for something—and when I look back toward Dorian, he's gone.

"Wait," I say, pressing myself against the glass. "Dorian, don't go—"

The music cuts off and I hear the faint sound of scratching.

A tug of memory. That scratching. That was the sound that made me first notice Dorian, the one that happened under my bed every night at—

I glance at the clock.

Midnight.

Dorian emerges from under the bed, but something's wrong. He twists and writhes across the floor like he's being dragged by someone I can't see. His fingertips scrabble against the floor, making that awful scratching sound. His mouth is open in a silent scream.

"Wh-what's happening?" I ask. "Something's wrong. Ezra—" I turn to him as he steps up beside me. "We have to do something!"

His expression is grim as he surveys the cell. "I wish we could."

"What do you mean?" I cry out as Dorian's mouth moves in an inaudible plea. He cowers on the floor, raising his hand against an invisible attacker. A blow sends him sprawling on his back. He tries to get up, but a weight presses him down again. His ribs compress as though under a crushing weight.

Ezra places a hand on my shoulder, but I wrench away. I don't understand how he can be so calm about this, why he isn't rushing into the cell to help Dorian right now.

"He's reliving his death," Ezra says. "It happens with ghosts. I know it's awful, I'm sorry, but he'll be okay afterward—"

I ignore him and slam my fist against the window. I can't stand here and watch this. I *refuse*. "Dorian," I cry. "*Dorian!*"

The desk beside us shudders as I scream, papers falling to the floor. The furniture inside of Dorian's cell shifts, too, as if blown back by a powerful force.

Dorian, one shaking hand still raised to defend himself, blinks out. Then he appears again, on his feet in front of the viewing window. Two of his arms wrap around his torso as he looks around, shaking his head. His chest rises and falls in a deep breath, and he reaches up, touching his mask as if reassuring himself it's still there. Then he looks at me and inclines his body in a graceful bow of thanks before disappearing again.

My legs go weak with relief. I sink to my knees on the tile.

"You...stopped it." Ezra stares down at me. "But...I've never... "

While he struggles for words, I pull my knees to my chest, struggling to calm my breathing. "He's done this before?"

"Yes. Most ghosts do at their time of death," Ezra says, still staring into the now-empty cell. "The first time you mentioned the scratching in your childhood, I thought that was why."

I swallow back revulsion as the realization hits me. *The scratching.* That's what was happening under my bed every night when I was a kid. He was reliving a horrible, painful death. "He didn't do it every night," I say. "Well, he did at the beginning, but then it stopped, until now…"

Ezra frowns. He turns away from the cell and looks at me. "Repetitive behavior is standard for ghosts. They're echoes of the past; they fall into old patterns. They don't…*change* like this." His brow furrows in thought. "But many things about Dorian aren't quite how a ghost behaves."

"I've been telling you," I whisper, "he's *different.*"

"But he behaved like a textbook poltergeist at the beginning," Ezra says, still staring at me, like *I'm* the puzzle here instead of Dorian. "And then…." Understanding breaks across his face. "Something changed him."

"What?" I ask, though I have an idea of what he's about to say. "You."

Chapter Sixteen

Ezra says he needs time to think, and I need time to rest. My head is still spinning from everything that's happened tonight, so I head home with his promise to alert me to any changes in Dorian's behavior and reconvene on Monday with a plan to move forward.

After being near Dorian once—feeling him, touching him, being held by him—I am empty without him. For the rest of the weekend I *ache* for him, alone in my house. Sometimes I crawl into bed and close my eyes and try to imagine him here, his body curled around mine. It soothes me in a way I haven't felt in a very long time.

Dorian. *My Dorian.* How could I have forgotten him? Now he plagues my thoughts like a craving. Like an obsession. He is mine and I am his, two halves of one heart, and it is painful to have been so close only to be ripped away from one another again.

It doesn't matter how he's changed, or what he's done. There is nothing he could do that I wouldn't be capable of forgiving. I am incomplete without him. I need him back, and I am willing to do whatever it takes to ensure it happens.

As I drift off to sleep, I feel a weight at my back. Fingers combing through my hair. Breath on my neck. It's almost like he's really here.

* * *

Making it through Sunday, knowing Dorian is in the cell waiting for me, is agonizing. I pace around the house, keeping myself busy with dusting and spot cleaning. It does little to calm the emotions that stir beneath my skin like an angry sea.

But my feelings aren't the only thing that have become volatile. I'm not sure if it was my contact with Dorian that awoke something in me, or if my emotions are doing it, but my once-subdued powers are roiling just beneath the surface now. When I reach for the duster, it leaps into my hand. When I try to make tea, the mug cracks in my hands, pieces of porcelain floating around me before tumbling to the floor.

Flashes of memory haunt me along with the surges of power. I see Dorian everywhere in fleeting recollections. Memories of him sitting on the counter beside me while I cook dinner, chasing me through the hallways in play, sleeping next to me in bed.

But that one important night is still a giant hole in my memory.

As I climb into bed, I squeeze my eyes shut and try to remember. I search my mind for any scraps about that night. My mother and father killed in front of me…how does one forget something like that? I had to have seen something, felt something, heard something.

When I strain, I can hear a whisper of something, just out of reach—

Step. Scraaape.

I blink, and suddenly, sunlight is streaming through the window.

"What?" I whisper. I raise a hand to rub my face and stop at the sight of dried blood coating my fingers. When I look down at myself, my once-white nightgown is a mess of rusty gore. I lurch out of bed and rush to the bathroom.

I pause at the sight of myself in the mirror: ghastly pale, with blood crusted over my nose and lips. As nauseating as it is, it floods me with relief.

A nosebleed. Just another nosebleed.

Still, I tremble through my shower, unable to banish the cold from my bones.

* * *

Ezra is seated at the table in the observation room when I arrive at the MRF on Monday, one long leg crossed over the other as he eyes his notes. But when he looks up, his hands go still halfway through the act of flipping a page.

"Are you all right?" he asks.

I nuzzle my nose deeper into my scarf. God, I hate the cold. "I'm fine." Except that I woke up as exhausted as though I hardly slept, even though I was out like a light. "How is Dorian?"

"His readings are holding steady," he says. "He hasn't made an appearance yet today, though."

I walk to the window and press my fingertips to the glass. Dorian flickers into visibility, sitting on the edge of the bed with all four arms folded over his chest and his lanky legs stretched out in front of him.

110

"There he is," I say, tapping a finger against the glass. Dorian stares at me, head tilting to one side, unreadable behind his mask.

"Hi," I breathe.

His mouth moves, but no sound comes out. I shake my head, but still, I can't wipe the smile off my face.

But then Dorian's gaze slides to Ezra at the desk next to me, and his eyes darken. He points at Ezra and then draws a finger across his own throat.

My heart stops. Is he saying that Ezra is a threat? But…when I was in the cell, Dorian pushed me *into* Ezra's arms. Surely he wouldn't have done that if he saw Ezra as dangerous.

I remember the crayon's scribbling—*MINE MINE MINE*—and suspect this acting out is because of something far more mundane: he's not used to sharing my attention. It was always just the two of us, back in the day.

"Stop that," I whisper to him.

"What's he doing?" Ezra asks, glancing up from his notes.

"Being rude," I mutter. Then I shift over to glance at his notebook, though I can't make much of his scribbled cursive. "Have you thought more about our next steps?" I'm nauseous at the thought of trying another hypnosis session, but if Ezra thinks that I'm the key to helping Dorian, then I'll brave it.

"Right." Ezra sets his notebook aside and gestures for me to sit across the table from him. "So, I have a theory. As you know, I've been struggling from the beginning to figure out what exactly Dorian *is*. Sometimes he behaves like a ghost. Sometimes he doesn't. I've spent a lot of time studying ghosts, classifying them, and I've never seen a haunting that behaves like he does."

I've never cared much about what Dorian is. All I care about is him being by my side. But maybe Ezra can offer insight into how to help him, so I listen.

"I think when you first met him, he *was* a poltergeist," Ezra says. "He was a child. He relived the moment of his death every night." I shiver at the reminder, casting a sad glance toward Dorian's cell. "But then he met you. That's when he got the mask, the four arms. He started to grow and change, which should be impossible for a ghost. He was no longer an echo of the past. He became something else. Something unique."

I nod. It makes sense, especially given what I've seen in my memories. As time went on, Dorian became stronger, more solid.

"So maybe I just need to spend time with him again?" I ask, stomach fluttering in nervous hope.

"I think it's more than that," Ezra says. "It shouldn't be possible for a human to affect a spirit like that. But...you and I both have some experience with impossible things."

He reaches across the table, his fingers brushing mine. Power sparks between us.

"I think your abilities are the key," he says, lowering his voice. "That's what brought him back from the brink the other night. It's what stopped him from reenacting his death, too. If you can learn to control them..."

That hopeful flutter in my stomach turns to an anxious twist. I swallow past a suddenly dry throat. Ezra is looking at me expectantly, but despite his enthusiasm, my stomach churns with dread. I've spent my entire life trying to subdue my powers, not control them.

"I—" I pull my hands into my lap and stare at them. "I don't know, Ezra. And isn't our goal to prove his innocence? I can't make him stronger just so he can spend his existence in that cell; it's not fair to him."

"I suspect your abilities are linked to your memory problems too," Ezra says. "I think you're blocking your own mind. Hurting yourself inadvertently when you go too deep into the hypnosis. Again, I think learning to control your abilities is the key to everything."

It's just a theory, but it makes sense. Still, the thought of using my powers *intentionally* makes me feel as though I'm teetering on the edge of a cliff. If I embrace that side of myself, will I ever be able to pretend to be normal again?

Plus, if the MRF finds out, we'll have even bigger problems. I could end up locked in the cell next to Dorian's instead of walking free with him.

"It's your choice," Ezra says. "But I think that controlling your abilities could help both you and Dorian. *You* are what brought him back. I think you can make him even stronger and protect yourself enough to find the truth in your memories." He looks at me. "Plus, Daisy…you deserve to live your life without being afraid of what you're capable of."

I think, again, of the looming question of that night I can't remember. I think of the table moving that day I couldn't suppress my anger, the way the room shook when I screamed in Dorian's cell. The sense of power seething and crawling beneath my skin, just waiting to be unleashed. "I don't know if it's possible not to be," I say quietly.

Ezra's gaze is steady. "Well, I think it is," he says. "And I'd like to prove it to you, if you'll let me."

My heart is in my throat. But I've come this far for Dorian; I can't stop now. So after a moment, I nod.

Chapter Seventeen

Walking into the MRF feels extra risky the next morning, knowing what we plan to do right under their noses. Ezra is waiting for me in the lobby with coffee, like he knows I need the boost. My hands tremble as I accept it from him, and he gives me a knowing, encouraging nod.

I'm exhausted after a sleepless night and terrified about potentially revealing my abilities to the MRF. But when I think of Dorian sitting in that cell, I find the courage to step through the door. Ezra and I walk toward the observation room.

"Ezra!"

We both freeze and turn as a smiling, dark-haired young woman approaches us from down the hallway.

"Hey, Mara," Ezra says. I stay at his side, unsure if I should speak, my eyes darting between the stranger and the observation room just a few steps away.

"Hey." The woman's eyes slide to me. "I don't think we've met! Are you new here? I'm Mara Vance."

I hesitate, clutching my coffee tighter.

"This is Gwen; she's a consultant on X-15," Ezra says.

"Ooh. Interesting. So are you a fellow, um, ghost enthusiast?"

"I guess you could say that," I mumble, fidgeting.

"Cool," she says. Then she peers at me more closely, and my discomfort grows. "You look familiar, actually. Do I know you from somewhere?"

Panic sparks in my chest and spreads, filling my body with an electric buzz of anxiety. "Oh, n-no, I don't think…" I glance up and meet her eyes and realize with a fresh wave of dread that I *do* recognize her. I have a vague memory of a younger version of her, chubby-cheeked with a gap between her teeth. She must be from Ash Valley. I didn't know her well, but it's a small town.

Her eyes widen in recognition, too, but she seems to note my frozen panic. She glances from me to Ezra, who gives the smallest shake of his head.

"Oh, my mistake. Never mind then," Mara says, with a breezy wave of her hand. "Anyway, lots to do, I'm off. But let's catch up soon, Ezra. I want to hear all the juicy details of what you've been up to." She shoots him a meaningful look, along with a finger gun.

"Sure, sure," he says, pushing his glasses up and giving her a grateful smile. When she leaves, he blows out a relieved breath. "She's a friend," he mutters. "Don't worry about her."

I nod, but my nerves are buzzing even more than before. Sometimes it seems like Ezra and I are the only ones in this building, but Mara is a reminder that that's not true. There are other people, and cameras, and so many ways for this to go wrong…

As I step into the observation room and see the equipment covering the table, I lurch to a stop, taken aback again.

"What is all of this stuff?" I ask, staring. There are strange metal devices heaped on the table and arranged on the floor.

Some of them look like medical tools, or something out of a science fiction movie. Others look more like torture devices. It's uncomfortably close to my memories of being institutionalized—or my nightmares about being locked in a lab and experimented on for the rest of my life.

Ezra smiles sheepishly. "Anything and everything that I thought might be helpful to us. As far as I could find by digging through the files, the MRF has never had access to a real psychic before, so there's no precedent about how to measure or evoke their abilities, aside from the tests I've done on myself over the years. We'll have to learn through trial and error."

I glance at the camera in the corner, noting that the blinking light is off as Ezra promised. Then I approach the table, eyeing the various bizarre machines.

But when I look toward the window into Dorian's cell, I know that I have to do this. He isn't visible right now, but I can *feel* him there—and I remember, too, the way I felt when I thought he was gone forever.

If using my abilities can strengthen Dorian, it is worth the risk. Even more so if Ezra is right that it will make it safe to explore my memories again and I can prove his innocence that way.

Or, if this all goes wrong and I need to break Dorian out myself... I suppose I'll need my abilities then, too.

Anyway, Ezra isn't some mad scientist who's going to go poking around in my brain. He's like me. "I trust you," I say, taking a seat.

I keep that in mind as I sit still while he attaches electrodes to my head, hooking me up to a machine. I swallow hard, hands fisting on my lap.

"This is just to measure your neural activity when you're using your powers," Ezra says. "It's not going to do anything to you, just take some readings that might be helpful in understanding the nature of your abilities."

"Okay," I whisper. "So, what now?"

He takes out a briefcase and sets a few objects out on the table between us: a deck of cards, a rubber ball, a few wooden blocks. Noticing my look, he says with a wry smile, "I'm reusing some of the items I initially gave Dorian to play with."

I reach out and take the ball, squeezing it in my grip. It reminds me of the one I once rolled under my bed as a child, my first peace offering to Dorian. Part of me wonders if he's played with this in his cell, if I might be able to feel some of his residual energy or presence on it. But it just seems like a normal ball.

"So what do you want me to do?" I ask.

"Try to use your powers," he says. "Any way you like."

He makes it sound so easy, but I've never *decided* to use my powers. It's just something that happens when my emotions run hot enough.

"I don't know how," I admit.

"There's no rush," Ezra says. "Just try. See what happens."

I nod. "Okay." I slowly unfurl my fingers from around the ball, letting it rest in the palm of my hand, and stare at it. I try to picture it rising into the air, hovering above my skin. When nothing happens, I focus harder, narrowing my eyes. I try to imagine a force coming from inside and pushing outward.

Still nothing.

I hold my breath until my face turns red. I focus so hard, I fear I'm about to burst a blood vessel. I envision the ball levitating a hundred times.

It doesn't move a centimeter.

After about thirty minutes of struggling, my shoulders slump, and I set the ball on the table.

"I can't do it," I say. "I'm sorry."

Ezra, who has been dutifully scribbling notes, gives me his ever-patient smile. "We both know that's not true," he says. "You definitely can. It's just a question of figuring out how to do it on command."

He's so warm and encouraging, but to my horror, tears of frustration and disappointment prick my eyes. I'm letting him down. Letting Dorian down. I wipe them away, embarrassed.

"Hey, none of that," Ezra says. "There's no pressure. This is day one."

"But I can't do anything, and it's just a stupid ball," I mumble.

"You're still the same girl who levitated a table. You can do this. We just have to figure out how you can activate it without those emotions doing it for you. "

* * *

Despite Ezra's optimism, the rest of the first day of testing proves useless. When I arrive the next morning, I'm still demoralized.

My first attempts to lift the ball again fail to provide anything of note. Trying not to get frustrated, I close my eyes and breathe. Ezra is quiet on the other side of the table, letting me concentrate. I focus on the air coming in and out of my lungs. The faint rattle of the air conditioning nearby. The sensation of Dorian's invisible presence in the room next door. When I focus and reach out with my senses, I'm more certain that he's there. Almost like I could see him if I opened my eyes. But I don't. Instead, I imagine reaching toward the glass—*through* the glass—to my old friend.

An invisible force nudges against my consciousness in return. The faintest brush of sensation against my mind, and something inside of me prickles into awareness in response. I remember sitting on my bedroom floor, reaching out and *pulling* my sketchbook into my hand with invisible force. I remember what it felt like, to access that power.

I slowly let my eyes open and set the ball I'm holding on the table. As I hold out an empty palm, I envision an invisible second hand growing from my arm, grabbing that ball, and pulling it toward me.

The ball flies off the table and straight into my grip.

I gasp in surprise and delight. It's such a small thing, but I'm grinning ear to ear as I look up at Ezra. "I did it!"

He smiles, pushing his glasses up with one finger. "Excellent," he says. "I think I got some interesting brain activity readings to look at. The EMF reader went off too."

Twenty minutes later, I have a ball consistently levitating above my palm. I stare at it as it slowly revolves in the air. It feels good, like stretching a long-neglected muscle. What else could I be capable of, if I learn to control it?

A sudden flash of memory, of the house rattling around me as I *scream*—

Thump. My concentration shatters as I jump in my chair. The ball drops to the table and rolls to the floor, and the memory slips through my fingers like sand. I turn and glare at the viewing window, where Dorian slams his fist into the window a second time. *Thump.*

He meets my eyes through the glass before disappearing.

"So much for him helping," I mutter, bending down to pick

up the ball from where it's fallen.

"Maybe he's feeling neglected," Ezra says. "That was good progress for today, anyway." He glances up from his notebook, and concern etches lines on his forehead. "Your nose is bleeding again."

"Oh." I wipe at it and see that he's right. "That happens."

"I hope we didn't push you too hard."

I wave a hand, unconcerned. "It's just a nosebleed. I feel fine."

"You had them when we explored your memories too. It could be a symptom of mental strain. Or your abilities working against you when you're stressed…"

I give him an exasperated look. "Or it's just a nosebleed. They've been happening all the time lately. Probably the dry air."

"Hmm." Ezra, looking unconvinced, scribbles again before shutting his notebook. "Well, regardless, it's a good place to call it a day. We made some progress."

"I guess." Levitating a ball hardly seems like a win, but it's better than nothing.

Ezra, at least, seems encouraged. "We'll try again tomorrow. Let me grab a tissue, and we can talk about next steps."

I nod and thank him, and the moment he's out of the room, I stand and walk to the viewing window. I stare into the next room, which appears empty once more, though I know Dorian is lurking somewhere.

"Why are you trying to sabotage me?" I whisper. "I'm trying to help us both."

I'm not sure if I'm talking to him or to myself. But either way, no answer comes.

Chapter Eighteen

Over the next couple of weeks, I slowly gain control of my abilities during my sessions with Ezra. It becomes easier to call upon them, until all it takes is a flicker of intent for me to lift an object above my hand.

I'm still not able to control anything larger than a few wooden blocks on command, even though I *know* I'm capable of lifting the entire table. Ezra is patient, but I'm irritated with myself.

More reassuring, however, is the fact that Dorian seems stronger as well. The more I use my powers, the more solid, more real, he seems to become. When we're practicing in the observation room, he spends more time visible than not, wandering restlessly in his cell while we do our tests. Sometimes he picks up the objects in his room in imitation of me, juggling wooden blocks when I lift them up, bouncing his ball against the glass while I levitate mine. I sense him watching through the window.

But whenever I try to speak with him, he disappears again.

It's becoming clear that Dorian is intentionally avoiding me, and it's driving me mad. It should be easy to get the truth about what happened from him. I wouldn't begrudge him if he managed to spin a convincing lie for Ezra and the MRF, but he doesn't do either of those things. It's like he doesn't *want* to be free.

Every morning, I arrive at the MRF with the hope that I'll have a breakthrough—with controlling my powers, remembering the truth, proving Dorian's innocence. But every evening, I leave disappointed and return to my empty house.

I find solace in the fact that progress continues there, too. Every evening, I continue practicing my powers until I'm too mentally exhausted to continue. And my memories are continuing to trickle in, as well. Just small things, moments and flashes of feelings around the house, but it's encouraging.

I'm leaning over the kitchen counter, reaching for a mug, when a memory hits me like a truck. A flash of me bending over the counter with Dorian behind me. His hard body pressed against my back, four hands gripping my hips, his mouth hot against my neck. I gasp at the vivid recollection, heat rushing to my face as I fumble with the mug. It slips from my hands—but with a flick of my wrist, I *catch* it mentally so it hovers a foot above the floor.

I bend down to pick it up and set it on the counter. I suck in a shaky breath and lean against the edge, trying to recall the sensation of that memory again. Even now, it leaves a lingering heat in my body. An ache between my thighs that I haven't felt in a long time.

I raise my fingers to my lips, remembering kissing Dorian in his cell. The sense that it had happened before. Clearly, much more than that happened between us.

Romance has never particularly interested me. Especially since I was always too scared to let anyone close. But maybe subconsciously I knew that it would be a betrayal to Dorian. Because he was more than just a friend back then, wasn't he?

He was my lover, too. He's the only one who has ever touched me like that. I didn't even realize how much I missed it.

I bite my lip and shut my eyes, reaching for that memory, or others like it. I want to remember what it felt like to be held and caressed. I recall the sensation of invisible fingers sliding through my hair, tugging lightly at the roots, and my head tilts back almost like I can really feel it now. A leg nudging my knees apart. More hands ghosting over my shoulders, down over my hips. Four hands, all for me…

"Made for you," Dorian's staticky voice whispers in my memory, before he licks a hot stripe up the side of my neck.

I grip the edge of the countertop with both hands as my legs wobble beneath me. A soft moan escapes me as I imagine a hand sliding under my nightdress from behind, pushing my panties to the side. I can almost feel it…

Suddenly, I'm bent over the counter, hips jerked back, and I *do* feel it. The sensation of my hands sliding over my skin even as they grip the counter. Fingers pushing inside of me, making me gasp and arch my back under an invisible weight. It feels too good for me to question what's happening. I'm helpless to do anything but whimper and grind my hips back, seeking it harder, deeper, *more*. I can only imagine what a desperate little thing I look like, bent over and rutting against nothing in my kitchen, but somehow the thought only stokes the flames inside of me. I'm already so wet and sensitive that all it takes is a few seconds for me to cry out, shaking and clutching at the counter as pleasure crests over me.

Then, just as quickly, it's gone. I'm left panting and weak, holding on to the kitchen counter to stay upright.

Alone.

Blinking, I press myself up straight again and reach down

to readjust my panties and pull down my nightgown. Did I just…masturbate with my powers? My already flushed face goes hotter still at the thought, and I press the back of my hand to my mouth to stifle an embarrassed laugh.

I guess relearning to control them does have *some* benefits. And not all of the memories this house holds are bad…

But many of them are. The house changes as the sun sets. The shadows grow longer, darker. I turn on every light in every room, but it never seems to reach the corners. The temperature drops, too. The dry cold of the desert in winter creeps through the walls and settles into my bones. Even wrapped in a blanket and armed with a mug of tea, I find it impossible to warm up.

As I climb the creaking stairs to my bedroom, I hear a sound behind me, almost like a crackle of static, or a whisper. When I turn to look over my shoulder, a memory hits me like a fist. I lurch off-balance as I recall a body lying at the bottom of the steps. I see limbs splayed, long hair in a halo on the floor, blood slowing pooling—*my mother?*—and myself, standing here …

I gasp, grabbing the railing to steady myself. A splash of red on the top stair gives me the disorienting sense that the memory has bled into the present. But then I blink and refocus and realize it's my own nose that's bleeding. I rush to the bathroom. As I wash my bloody hands in the sink, that, too, gives me a queasy, alarming sense of déjà vu.

I crawl into bed, but I find no escape in my dreams.

"Daisy." My mother's voice is a harsh, painful wheeze, barely recognizable. Dread churns my stomach as I turn to face her. A part of me already knows what I'll see, but that doesn't stop it from being a gut punch. She stands a foot away from the bed with her back bent at a horrible angle and blood running from the corners of her eyes, which are fixed on me. "Daisy, what have you done?"

I whimper, crawling across the bed away from her. "I didn't… I don't…"

She takes a step closer, reaching for me. But when she grabs my arm, the flesh melts from her fingers, leaving only skeletal claws digging into my skin. "Why, Daisy? Why?"

I yank free from her grip, shaking my head, and back away into something solid. I shriek and whip around, and there's my father at the foot of the bed, his face twisted in fury. He grabs my ankle and yanks me toward him. When he opens his mouth, I expect him to shout, but instead, only a horrible gurgle and a rush of blood comes out. It drips down his chin and over his shirt, puddling at his feet. His face splits down the middle into an awful, gaping wound.

"No," I groan. "Please…"

"Daisy, why?" my mother asks again.

I yank my foot free and retreat from both of them. "Please, leave me alone, I…" But when I raise my hands to cover my ears to block out their accusations and horrible sounds, they stick to my skin, damp and tacky. I jerk in surprise and then stare down at my own hands in horror.

They're covered in blood.

* * *

I wake with a gasp, and it takes me a disoriented moment to realize why the room looks different. It's because I'm floating in the air. My bed is suspended beneath me, along with the nightstand, and the lamp. Everything in the room is levitating lazily, as if gravity has been turned off. But as soon as I realize

125

it, panic grips me, and everything falls. Including me.

The bed hits the floorboards with a *thump*, and I hit it half a second later, bouncing off the mattress. The nightstand topples over, sending my glass of water to the floor; it shatters. The lamp hits the floor and flickers out, bathing the room in darkness.

I catch a glimpse of movement in the shadows. A pair of eyes, watching me. But I blink and they're gone, and the scream dies in my throat.

I sit stunned, clutching my bedsheets and trying to breathe normally. Cold sweat clings to my skin. I swallow thickly, release my grip on my blanket, and push my hair out of my face. *Just a nightmare*, I tell myself, but I'm not sure I believe it. It isn't just a nightmare when it might be a glimpse into my lost memories, or a side effect of my developing abilities.

It's impossible to know if I should be afraid when I can't even trust my own mind anymore.

Chapter Nineteen

The next day, Ezra is pacing in the observation room when I enter, hair askew from running his fingers through it. He stops when he sees me and offers a smile that's strained around the edges.

"You look tired," he says.

"So do you," I say, studying the shadows under his eyes.

"I have a meeting with Dr. Wright and the director today," he says. "You can stay here, practice your abilities, or speak to Dorian through the panel if you want."

I can't deny I'm eager for a chance to be alone with Dorian, but the tension in his expression unsettles me. I've always been hypervigilant about noticing such things, and now, it's like a prickle of alarm under my skin. "Is something wrong?"

His gaze darts away from mine. One of his shoes taps against the tile. "No. I don't think so."

His anxiety is contagious; now it's pooling in my gut as well. "You don't think they know what we've been doing? Did they notice the camera being turned off?"

"If they knew I was carrying out unapproved experiments in one of their labs, I'm sure they'd be here this very second, shutting us down."

Despite his words, he doesn't look convinced. "Then…?"

"I don't know what they want, but I'm sure it's no big deal. Just…wait here for me." He gestures with one hand, a calming motion. "I should be back in about an hour."

"Okay," I say, my stomach coiled in knots.

As he turns to walk out the door, I act on instinct. My hand juts out at my side, and I *pull*.

When the door clicks shut behind Ezra, I'm left alone in the observation room with his MRF ID clutched in my palm. My heart is pounding, and I'm sure he'll check his pocket and realize that it's empty…but a minute ticks by, and nothing happens.

I glance at the camera to verify that it's still shut off, and clutch the card hard enough that the plastic bends. This is risky. And wrong. I'm betraying Ezra's trust, and I could get him in trouble with his superiors, but I can't shake the worry that he's *already* in trouble, despite his denials. Maybe his superiors are already onto us, and maybe they're not. Either way, this may be my only chance to see Dorian face-to-face unsupervised.

But as I step outside, I come to a stop, my eyes finding the camera in the corner of the hallway. I'm sure there's another one in his cell. Am I willing to risk everything to see him? This could be my last chance.

What if I ruin any shot at Dorian being released from this place?

While I'm still standing, torn by indecision, footsteps approach.

"Gwen?"

I turn to see Ezra's friend, Mara, approaching with concern etched on her face. I shove Ezra's keycard into my pocket.

"Is everything all right?" she asks.

"Yes," I say, but my voice cracks and my eyes well with tears before I can stop it. I'm so tired of keeping everything inside, pretending everything is okay. But it's humiliating to break down like this in front of a near stranger. "Well, no. I-I…" I stare hopelessly at the doorway to Dorian's cell, the keycard burning a hole in my pocket. I'm so close to him, closer than I've ever been, but still not close enough.

Mara follows my gaze to the door, and her expression turns sympathetic. "I see," she murmurs. "Believe it or not, I may know how you feel."

"Did Ezra tell you about what we're doing?" I ask, hope and dread waging war in my churning stomach.

"He didn't tell me much about you. But he told me about Dorian. I said I'd help if I could."

"Then help me," I burst out before I can second-guess myself. "I need to see him. Privately."

Mara hesitates. "I…might be able to help with that, but…"

"Please," I beg.

She glances up and down the hallway, wets her lips. "Okay," she says. "I can get you a few minutes." She moves her hands in sudden, rapid hand movements I recognize as sign language but can't understand. Then my attention snags on her shadow cast on the wall behind her. It's moving, too—but I swear the motions are delayed, and *different*, than what she's doing with her hand.

As soon as I blink, it's back to normal, and I'm not sure if I imagined the whole thing.

"Wait two minutes," Mara says. "Then do what you need to do."

"Thank you," I whisper.

"You're welcome." Her lips twinge. "Daisy."

* * *

Two minutes later, I hold my breath as I swipe Ezra's keycard—and the door opens with a beep. My heart hammers in my ears as I step through.

But the second door holds firm when I tug on the handle. There's no keypad here, nothing but a blank metal door. My heart stops—but I remember watching Ezra come through here, and thinking it was like an airlock. When I shut the external door behind me, the inner one clicks open.

Then there is nothing stopping me from stepping into Dorian's cell.

I turn in a circle, taking in the entire room. I'm struck again by how tiny it is. I closed the shutters and turned off the viewing window's opacity before leaving the observation room so even that is gone, leaving what appears to be a normal mirror.

And Dorian is nowhere to be found. Avoiding me even now.

"Dorian," I say. "It's just me. I want to talk."

A moment passes. He doesn't appear.

Frustration pricks me. "I know you're here. Show yourself!"

I'm still turning to search the room, but I jerk to a stop as he appears. He's suddenly standing in front of me, looking down from behind his mask. I step toward him, and he steps back. He folds all four arms over his chest and tilts his head toward the door behind me.

"Really?" I clench my jaw, teeth grinding in frustration. "I'm not leaving here until you explain what's going on." I step closer, and he steps back. I circle around him, forcing him to turn to watch me. As if *he's* the one who needs to be wary here. "Why are you avoiding me? Ezra and I are trying to help you—" His eyes flash behind the mask, and I pause. "What? *Ezra?*" He turns his head. "Has he done something?"

Dorian gives the tiniest shake of his head, like he loathes to admit it.

I sigh. Relieved, despite myself. "So you're just…what?" I stop circling, one hand on my hip. "Are you *jealous* of him?"

With his head still turned away from me, I can see the hard line of Dorian's jaw as he clenches it.

"You're ridiculous," I whisper. I feel ridiculous too, having a conversation out loud by myself, but when we're this close, it's like we don't need to talk. "There's nothing between me and Ezra." Dorian turns back to me, rolls his eyes behind the mask. "Fine, there's something, but we're just *friends.*"

His eyes darken.

"I *am* allowed to have other friends."

He is radiating silent fury. But when I step closer, he doesn't retreat this time. I reach out and grab the front of his suit, digging my fingers into the fabric. Real, *solid* fabric bunched in my hand.

"But you and I are something different," I say. "Something more. I remember enough to know that." I search his eyes, so very dark behind the mask, his pupils huge and black and locked on me. All four hands clench like he's physically holding himself back from touching me.

Why?

"Just tell me what's going on," I beg. "Tell me what to do."

He reaches with one gloved hand to touch my face, but when I lean into the feather-soft contact, he pulls away. Another hand points at the door behind me.

"I'm not going anywhere without you," I say. The words taste familiar. "I'm not afraid of the MRF. I'm getting my powers back. And my memories."

The lights flicker above us. A burst of static comes from the radio. I glance at it, and then back at Dorian—and his hands wrap around my throat. He forces me backward until I hit the wall, and leans in close, his mask brushing my nose.

"It's not them you should be afraid of," he whispers, his voice coming both from behind the mask and the radio, dark, distorted.

I smile, even with his gloved hands wrapped around my throat. I tilt my head back, surrendering to him.

"Are you trying to scare me away?" I ask. "It's too late for that."

His grip on me goes slack. I wrap my arms around him before he can pull away. He rears back, but I hold him close. After a second he gives in, shoulders slumping, mask resting against my forehead.

"My Dorian," I murmur. He's so warm and solid against me. I hadn't realized until now how long it's been since anyone touched me. I arch against him, pulling him closer, asking for *more, more.*

There is an answering desperation in his touch. One of his hands grips the back of my head in a possessive motion; two others slide down over my hips. The last still grips my throat, but it's more of a caress than a threat.

"Dorian," I say, lower this time, hoarse, a plea. I'm not sure what I'm asking for, but he seems to know.

He lifts me, carrying me to the table. In the mirror behind him, I see only the reflection of myself sitting on the edge with my legs spread and my dress rucked up around my waist. Mortified, I move to close them, but Dorian is standing between them, making it impossible.

This isn't what I came here for. There is so much I need to talk to him about, to understand why he's acting like this, to form a plan to help him escape. But…he is so close, and I've missed this so very much.

"We shouldn't," I whisper. But as Dorian leans closer, I tilt my head back, lips parting, opening myself to him.

Dorian lifts his mask just enough that he can kiss me. It's hesitant at first, but when I kiss back, he grips me harder, kisses me more deeply. Urgently.

"My Dorian," I say again, my fingers digging into the muscles of his back. He groans at the sound of his name in my mouth and kisses me again, his tongue moving against mine. Two of his hands caress my breasts while the other two slide up my thighs. My skin is hot and sensitive, each touch making me whimper. My power sizzles beneath my skin—and when Dorian kisses me again, it flows through me and *into* him. His body feels harder, hotter, as he grinds against me.

As his mouth moves down to my neck, I catch another glimpse of myself in the mirror behind him. My hair is askew and my lips parted as I pant. As Dorian bites a sensitive spot on my neck, I cry out and watch through heavily lidded eyes as the red marks appear on my skin. God, it's hot, watching myself be ravished like this.

I feel so held, so cherished in his arms, yet still I want more. I want all of him. I want to show him that all of me still belongs to him. I want to know that our bodies still fit like we were made for each other.

Right now, I don't care about how I look in the mirror, or about Ezra finding out about this, or even whether or not Dorian is a murderer. Because I have never felt anything as right as being held by him. This is how it was. This is how it should be. The two of us, forever entwined, never to be separated.

"I miss you so much," I groan as his tongue trails down my neck. I missed him before I remembered him. Even when I thought I was insane, I could feel that a piece of myself was missing, and here it is. *Dorian, my Dorian.*

He breathes against my skin, inhales the scent of me, and then rips my panties straight off. He crumples them in his fist and shoves them into his pocket before I can protest. "You have no idea," he whispers through the radio as his fingers slide inside of me. I can feel the heat of him through the leather gloves. His voice is so much clearer now, barely a crackle of static to it. "I thought of you every day, every minute, every second. Even when I didn't know myself, I knew you."

I whimper as his fingers work inside of me, stretching me out, effortlessly finding the spot that makes me gasp and writhe. "Take me," I say. "Take all of me, I'm yours."

"Mine," he echoes. Two of his hands pull off his belt while he continues to fuck me slowly with his fingers. I fumble with his buttons as he kicks his shoes off. Soon he's long and lean and gloriously naked over me, except for his mask and his gloves. He pulls his fingers out of me, and my whimper of protest dies away as a long tongue slides out of the hole in his mask to lick them clean.

My gaze darts between his mouth and his cock—

Cocks, that is.

I blink, a strangled noise escaping me as I take in the sight. Two cocks, both of them hard and ready and terrifying in their size. I don't know why that shocks me more than the four arms, except that I know that every time his body has changed, it's been—

"For me," I whisper, wrapping a hand around one thick shaft

and giving him an experimental stroke. Dorian gasps, thrusting into my hand.

"Always," he pants through the radio. "Only for you."

I bite back a whimper as I reach with my other hand to stroke both of his lengths at once. He grips the table so hard, the metal groans, his head falling forward and his eyes shutting in bliss.

"I've always been everything you need," he pants. "*All* that you need."

"Yes," I whisper, drinking in the sound of his voice, the sight of his pleasure.

But when he opens his eyes and looks down at me, there's a vulnerability in his gaze, too.

"You still are," I promise him, realizing what he's after. "You're the only one. Always and forever."

"Tell me he's nothing."

It takes me a moment to remember who he's even talking about. "He's nothing," I say, burying a hint of guilt as I think of Ezra's late nights helping me, everything he's risking for us.

"I hate watching him with you," Dorian confesses, a raw note in his voice that makes him sound more human than ever. "While I'm trapped in here— While I can't—"

"Stop it." I squeeze both of his cocks hard enough that he grunts in surprise, hips jerking. I look up at him, holding his gaze. "Stop talking about him. I'm here. This is about us."

He breathes shakily. Nods.

But just as I'm finding a rhythm again, Dorian pushes my hands away and spreads my thighs, lining one of those stiff lengths up with the wet heat of my core. He strokes the other slowly.

My breath hitches. I want this so badly, I'm dripping for it, but still… "You're so big," I whisper. "I don't know if I can…"

"You can take me," he promises, before I can even finish. He lifts my chin with one finger, looking me in the eyes. But though he said it like a fact, there's a question in his gaze.

I swallow and nod. I always thought I was a virgin, but… there's a sense of rightness, a flicker of familiarity, as he slides the head of his cock against my slick need. My body remembers him, even though our past is lost to the void of my memories.

And of course, how could Dorian be anything but perfect for me?

I tremble and arch as his fingers slide down the notches of my spine. My legs part wider, ready for him.

He yanks me to the edge of the table, and then he's pushing against me, working himself into me inch by inch, stretching me out until I am full to the brim.

A perfect fit. Like he was—

"Made for me," I gasp, clutching him. Of course he is. Every piece of him is designed to give me what I need. Four strong arms to hold me, two perfect cocks to please me.

I cry out, digging my nails into his shoulders as he fucks me slow and deep, pressing me into the table. I claw at his back, whimper his name. His hands are all over me, caressing and gripping me, all four sliding over my ass, my breasts, my hips. We are caught somewhere between a feral need and an aching tenderness. When tears gather in the corners of my eyes, he licks them away—then at the trickle of blood sliding down from my nose to my upper lip. He shudders at the taste of me.

As his pace increases, he lifts me off the table, holding me effortlessly in the air as he thrusts inside of me. I catch a glimpse of myself in the mirror again, and I look— *God.* I look unhinged, possessed, otherworldly. Then Dorian turns me and pushes me against the mirror, fucking me against it so I look up and see him, and only him, his eyes dark and intense behind the white mask. His other cock slides against my clit as he thrusts, and my eyes roll back in pleasure. As my fingers dig into his muscular back, I know—I *know* with absolute certainty—that he has held me just like this, fucked me just like this.

And I somehow forgot.

My heart aches as I hold him. Even as he ruts against me and gasps my name, even as my body pulses and trembles through another orgasm right along with him, I cannot ignore the sense that something important is missing. I miss him even when we're skin to skin, even when he's still deep inside me. Even as he pulls out only to thrust his second cock into me, filling me up again, I gasp and plead for more.

Tears slide down my cheeks as I press my face into his shoulder.

Dorian pulls out of me, leaving me aching and empty, and sets me down on the floor.

Two hands still hold me steady as the others grip my face and lift it toward his, gentle and questioning. I squeeze my thighs together as I feel him dripping out of me, desperate to hold on to any piece of him I can get.

"How could I forget you?" I ask, my voice trembling. "How could I ever forget?"

Even without seeing his face, I sense him shift. He pulls away from my touch, turns his masked face from me. When he releases me and steps back, I teeter on my feet, leaning against the window for support.

"You mustn't remember," he whispers through the radio, and presses a hand to his heart. "Trust me, Daisy. And *leave me*."

"No." I wipe at my tears, furious at my weakness. "We can leave right now. Let's find a way together." I don't have to remember everything to know that I want him walking out of here with me. "I don't care what you've done—what *we've* done. We belong together."

"You're safer without me," he says.

Before I can open my mouth to refute it, he disappears. And no matter how much I cry and shout for him, he doesn't come back.

* * *

Ezra finds me slumped at the table in the observation room, head in my hands. I lift it to look at him as he walks in. I hid his keycard among his files on the table and spent a while cleaning up in the bathroom, fixing my rumpled clothes and wild hair, washing my face and between my thighs. Still, it feels like my guilt is written all over my skin, like every place Dorian's hands and mouth touched me must glow like red brands of condemnation. I am humiliatingly aware of my bareness beneath my skirt, the throbbing soreness between my thighs.

But Ezra seems like he's hardly able to look at me anyway. His head is low, his eyes on the floor.

I sit up. "What's wrong? What did they say?"

He pushes his glasses up to massage the bridge of his nose. "They think I've been spending too much time working with Dorian. That I should place more focus on my other subjects."

My heart sinks. "But Dorian needs you." *We need you.*

Ezra shrugs. "They don't see it that way. Dr. Wright is angry that I haven't encouraged Dorian to pass on, and I couldn't come up with a good excuse without revealing everything." He looks at me. "She and Director Ramsey still believe he murdered your parents, so they're not even considering rehabilitation. Therefore, he's a lost cause."

My lower lip trembles. "But that's not true."

"I don't know that for sure. Neither do you. And he won't cooperate."

I open my mouth, shut it again. "We can't give up now," I say in a quiet voice. "Let's…" I pause, swallow. Think of Dorian saying "you mustn't remember." Warning me of *danger*. "Let's do one more memory retrieval. Let's go back to that night."

He blinks at me, surprised. His mouth works for a moment before he says, "I'm not sure if you're ready for that."

"I might never be ready," I say. "But I need to know."

Ezra searches my face, and I feel laid bare in front of him. "Did something happen?"

"I just…" Should I tell him the truth? But I'm not even sure what the truth is. I don't know how to express the jumble of fears inside of me, the nightmares that have been keeping me up at night, the weird occurrences around me and my unpredictable powers. If I try, I'm scared I'll just sound crazy.

I trust Ezra, but I know it would put him in a difficult position if I admit that my powers are getting out of control. If I told him I think I might be a danger to myself and others, would he continue to let me walk around town freely? Or would he lock me up in the MRF, just another one of his subjects?

Tears of frustration sting the corners of my eyes, and I blink them away, turning to gaze through Dorian's viewing window instead of looking Ezra in the eyes. "It's…so hard for me, being this close to Dorian but not being able to really be with him."

"I understand." The sympathy in Ezra's tone makes my stomach twist with guilt. "But we can't rush this. Like I said, I want Dorian to be free, but I want to do it *officially*. There was an incident, with X-14, that shook peoples' faith in our new leadership, but I think this can restore it and pave a path for the future. I'm sure I can convince Dr. Wright and the Director, given time. But that means we have to be *extremely* careful about this. Not just for Dorian, but for all of the other patients that will come after. That's why I've been so careful this whole time. We have to do this the right way."

Another wave of guilt churns my stomach, but I swallow it. I hadn't thought about what this means for the other patients. I can only afford to think about Dorian. I have to do what's right for him.

I feel the same flicker of guilt I did in the cell, when I told Dorian that Ezra was *nothing*. Maybe I meant it more than I thought.

Chapter Twenty

y nose bleeds on and off the entire drive back from the MRF. Fractured memories assault my mind, making it hard to focus on the road. Being so close to Dorian must have cracked the dam. Now I see: Dorian pushing his mask up to kiss me in the garden. Dorian holding me from behind while I brew tea in the kitchen, his chin resting on the top of my head. Dorian above me in bed, our breaths mingled, tangled in sweat-slick sheets.

He was my lover. My first and only. *How could I have forgotten?*

By the time I make it home, I'm lightheaded, my face crusted with blood. I stumble up the steps to the front door, fumble with numb fingers to discard my coat and boots, and head straight to a bath.

Scrubbing the dried blood off me helps. But I can still feel the imprint of Dorian's fingers on my skin. What happened today was a mistake. A betrayal of Ezra's trust. And it's left me more confused than ever.

Another memory flashes through my mind like a burst of lightning—this one from one of our hypnosis sessions. The one of invisible hands holding me underwater in this very bath until it felt like my lungs would burst.

I shiver, suddenly cold despite the steaming water, and pull my knees to my chest. I still can't make sense of that, or Dorian's insistence on pushing me away. The more I think about it, the more I try to put together my splintered memories, the more my head aches.

A drop of red falls in the water and slowly disperses. My nose is bleeding again.

Between the blood loss, my headache, and the steam filling the room, I'm too foggy and exhausted to do anything about it. I just watch as blood drips, drips, drips into the bath, turning the water a murky pink. My eyes drift past it, over the edge of the porcelain tub, to the fogged-up mirror beyond. Red flashes in my reflection—not dripping from my nose, but glowing in my eyes.

I blink, scrub a hand over my face, and it's gone.

God, I'm really losing it.

I sigh and shut my eyes, letting my hand drift down over my mouth. My fingers smear blood over my lips, down my neck. They continue to drift between my breasts, over my stomach. My knees slide apart. As my thoughts blur, my head lolls back against the side of the tub, and my hand moves toward the apex of my thighs, where I'm still sore from my tryst with Dorian.

What am I doing?

I watch my blurred reflection in the mirror through heavily lidded eyes. My own hand strokes over my achingly sensitive core beneath the blood-tinged water. I let my eyes slide shut, my soft whimpers filling the room. I'm already sore, but a little bit of pain only seems to heighten the pleasure.

I come so hard it hurts, clenched around my fingers—and for a heartbeat, I feel hot breath against my ears, a larger hand wrapped around my own, urging my motions. I try to scream, but I can't move—can't do anything as I slowly slide into the tub, until my head slips beneath the surface of the water—

Then I sit up, coughing and gasping, suddenly in control of my body again. I rake wet hair out of my face and drag myself out of the tub and over to the mirror. I smear a hand through the foggy condensation and stare into my reflection, but there are only my own wide blue eyes looking back at me. I touch my face, my lips, searching for some sign of anything alien.

But there is only me. Was that a dream? Another memory surfacing? Or…is it possible it was something else entirely?

* * *

A realization is creeping up on me.

The memories I've uncovered…the nightmares…the nose-bleeds. That piece of paper under the bed. The music I hear sometimes in the middle of the night. The *cold* in this house, something deeper than a winter chill.

I've been writing off these odd coincidences as side effects of my burgeoning abilities. But what if there's something else at work here?

What if there has been something else in the house with me this entire time?

Ezra mentioned that people with abilities like ours attract attention from spirits. It's probably what drew Dorian to me in the first place when we were both young. So, then, is it possible he wasn't the only thing haunting this house? Could there be another spirit? Maybe more than one?

Goose bumps prickle over me. That thought fills me with such cold dread that I have an urge to flee the house and never return. I can think of few things more horrible than looking into a mirror one day and seeing the ghostly visage of my father looming over my shoulder, or my mother's pale, cruel hands reaching toward me.

But whatever just happened in the bathroom wasn't one of them. So how do I find out who it is?

Back when I was a child, Dorian reached out to me on his own. But this time, I may have to be the one who makes contact. I know little about the art of dealing with spirits, despite my background and my abilities. I'm certain I could ask Ezra, but I'm not sure I'm ready to invite any follow-up questions from him quite yet. I've already asked so much of him, anyway. If I'm certain that a ghost is here, I'll ask him for assistance in dealing with that—and laying them to rest. But this is a shot in the dark, and there's no sense in wasting his time and making him question my sanity any more than he surely already has.

So I'm forced to resort to a quick internet search and a trip to a local store.

It's rather humiliating, buying a Ouija board as a grown woman. The cashier gives me a dry look and comments, "Isn't it a little late for Halloween?"

It doesn't feel so childish, though, when I'm alone in my living room with the board set out in front of me. I remember hearing of kids playing with these things back in the day, but of course my parents would never allow such a thing in the house. And it wasn't as though I had any friends to do it with, anyway, except for Dorian.

I don't have anyone I trust now, either. So it's just me, alone in my empty old house, placing two fingers on the planchette.

Foreboding sweeps over me, but I shake it off. This is just a piece of plastic. I doubt there's anything inherently paranormal about it, but with my powers to assist, it may prove to be a useful tool.

I think of Ezra's words during our hypnosis sessions: *Focus your mind. Shape your intent.*

"I want to make contact with the other side," I whisper, letting my eyes slide shut. And then, more loudly, I say, "Is anyone there? Can you hear me?"

There's nothing but the soft creaks and groans of the house settling around me. The familiar noises of a place that is very old and very empty. The planchette remains still under my fingers.

I'm not sure if I'm more disappointed or relieved, but I'm not ready to give up quite yet and leave my—fears? hopes?—*suspicions* to rest.

"It's Daisy," I say to the empty house. "I came back. I'm looking for answers. If you're here, then…please, talk to me." I pause, swallowing a lump in my throat. "Please, answer. Is there anyone here?"

Silence lingers in the aftermath of the question. But suddenly there's pressure on my fingers, like another hand on top of mine, guiding it. My eyes fly open with a gasp, tracing the movement of the plastic as it slides around the board and lands on the word *YES*.

"Hi," I whisper, uncertainty twinging in my gut. I guess, after all this, I wasn't really expecting an answer. Dread and relief mingle in my stomach, setting my nerves alight. "Who am I speaking to?"

There's no response.

"You don't have to be afraid," I say. "I want to help you. Please, can you tell me your name?"

Still, there's nothing.

I don't know much about ghosts, but it's possible it doesn't remember its name. Maybe its presence is weak, like Dorian when I first came back to Ash Valley.

"I lived in this house when I was a child," I say. "Have you been here since then?"

The planchette circles *YES* again.

I bite my lip. "I've...forgotten some things since then," I say. "Have we met before?"

Another *YES*.

"Oh." I take a breath, try to think back on my recovered memories. Everything is so scattered still; I'm struggling to put the pieces into a coherent picture, or into a timeline. "Do you know Dorian?"

Another *YES*. But the planchette doesn't stop there this time; it keeps sliding, spelling out words. The blur of letters is almost too fast to understand. *Almost*. But as it finishes, my stomach drops like a stone.

I KILLED HIM.

I try to pull my fingers off the planchette, but I physically can't. The weight on the back of my hand increases until it's almost painful, until the plastic slides out from under me and it's just my fingers pressed against the Ouija board. I can feel someone or something holding me in an ironlike grip.

"What do you want?" I cry out, tears forming in my eyes as I try to resist.

This weight, this *thing*, drags my hand across the board in lieu of the planchette, touching the letters with my own two fingers in an act that is invasive, revolting, a betrayal of my autonomy.

But the message is almost more horrifying than that.

LET ME OUT.

A small, terrified gasp slips out of me as I remember Ezra's warnings about people like us being especially prone to possession. Does this thing want to use me as a way out of the house?

I refuse to let that happen. I am not some helpless girl, some *thing* to be used.

Now that I know how to do it, it's easy to call up my power. I draw it around me like a cloak, imagining a protective barrier that settles over my skin.

"Leave me alone," I shout, and push the barrier *out*.

A gust of wind sends the discarded planchette tumbling end over end, making the walls tremble. There's a *pop* of pressure, and wet warmth bursts from my nose.

I shriek and cover my face, startled by the force of it, and only then realize that I'm free to move my hand again. The disembodied pressure is gone. I can't feel the presence here anymore. I cradle my hand to my chest, shivering, and when I look down, red marks in the shape of fingerprints ring my wrist.

Chapter Twenty-One

I call Ezra and wait on the porch, trying to staunch my nosebleed. This is a particularly bad one, rendering me lightheaded and foggy. My wrist throbs, too; the red marks have now darkened into visible bruises.

Soon, Ezra pulls into the driveway and emerges with an armful of ghost-hunting equipment. But he sets it aside to pull me into a hug and then steps back to look me over.

"Are you all right?"

"I'm fine," I say with a weak smile.

"Thank God," he mutters. "Ouija boards are nothing to mess with, Daisy, especially for people like us." He grabs his equipment again. "Stay here while I have a look around."

I grab his arm before he can enter the house. "Wait," I say. "I-I-I don't think it's safe in there. Let me come with you."

He smiles, gently removes my hand. "I've dealt with hauntings before. I'll be all right, I promise."

And so I end up on the porch, unable to do anything but shiver and wait. Five minutes pass, and then ten.

Finally, I can't take it anymore.

I pull the door open and hesitate there, staring into the foyer. It's quiet and still. Deceptively normal. "Ezra?" I call, and step inside.

The silence is deeper than usual. There are none of the usual creaks and groans, like even the house is holding its breath. My steps seem to echo faintly as I move forward.

"Ezra?" I call out again, louder.

The lightbulb above flickers—and then shatters, plunging the room into darkness. I shriek as glass rains down around me, and I retreat toward the door—but it slams shut behind me.

"*Ezra!*" I shriek again, panicked this time. I grab the handle and pull, but it's stuck. I try to reach for my powers, but my fear is too overwhelming, making it difficult to concentrate.

Something is breathing in the darkness behind me.

I whirl around, pressing my back to the door, and choke on a frightened sob. Blood flows steadily from my nose, dripping over my lips and down my chin. "Leave me alone!"

Footsteps thud down the stairs, and I am frozen, stuck between running toward them or away—but when a warm hand grips mine and that familiar connection sparks, I immediately know that it's Ezra. The EMF reader in his other hand is going haywire, the meter a bright, dangerous red: *Maximum activity.*

Ezra drops the reader on the floor, providing a dim illumination, and reaches for something else. "Salt and iron," he mutters under his breath. "Maybe just salt will hold it off—" He pulls out a salt shaker and spills it on the floor around us.

I wipe my hand over my still-bleeding nose and flick it over the salt. It's not much iron, but maybe—

The EMF dies. Ezra and I are both still, clutching each other and breathing fast. Then I fumble for the handle behind me, and the door creaks open without resistance.

We both race to Ezra's car. I curl up in the passenger seat, one hand pressed to my nose to staunch the flow. Ezra reverses out of the driveway hard enough to make me lurch in my seat and stops only when we're past the gate.

I hug my knees to my chest, heart pounding in my ears and blood still dripping between my fingers.

"Jesus." Ezra runs shaky fingers through his hair. "I...I couldn't find anything at first. I wasn't getting any readings until you stepped into the house, but the *strength* of that reaction to your presence..."

As terrifying as the experience was, something like elation bubbles up inside me.

"Did you check the attic?" I ask.

"I was about to when I heard you call for me."

I knew it. I smile, triumphant. "Do you understand what this means?"

Ezra frowns at my expression. I imagine how I must look—blood dripping from my nose, grinning like a maniac—and try to control myself. "That you're in danger," he says. "I've only felt this kind of malevolence once before, Daisy. It's..." He shakes his head, sucking in a shuddering breath. "You remember how I told you that some spirits can warp over time? Turn malicious? That's what it feels like. They become something that most of us would call a *demon.*"

I pause at the word "demon," fear flickering through me, but still I cling to my original thought. "Okay, but it also means there's another possibility we haven't thought about." He tilts his head, clearly not understanding, so I continue. "It means maybe it wasn't Dorian *or* me that killed my parents that night. There's someone—or something—else in the house. It was already there back then. It *must* be the one responsible."

And maybe *it's* the thing that was haunting me in those confusing old memories. The rules hidden under my mattress:

Don't look at it. Don't think about it. Ezra *told* me that attention is how spirits gain strength.

Ezra's frown is thoughtful but still troubled. "If that's the case, why wouldn't Dorian tell us?"

My shoulders slump. "I don't know," I admit. "Maybe he's scared of it. He did say it was dangerous for me to remember."

A strange expression crosses Ezra's face. "When did he say that?"

I pause, realizing my mistake. "During one of our sessions? When else?"

Ezra shakes his head. "I would've remembered that," he says. "I never would've entertained the thought of doing more memory retrieval attempts if that was the case."

"But we have to!" I lean forward, desperate for him to understand. "Don't you see? This is our chance to prove that Dorian is innocent. To argue for his release. Isn't that what you want?"

"Of course it is," Ezra says. "But not if it puts you in danger. We both know what happens when you push too hard to regain your memories. You almost drowned. Maybe that's what Dorian was warning you about when he told you it was dangerous." He glances at me again, brow furrowed, and I know that he still doesn't quite believe me about when Dorian said that to me.

"Then let me ask him about it," I say. "Face-to-face. This isn't the sort of thing I can discuss with him through a plane of glass with the cameras on."

Ezra shakes his head. "You know I can't sanction that," he says. "And it's too risky. We have to do this right if we want to get him released. We have to be patient, for the sake of the future of the MRF and all of the other subjects there."

Frustration boils in my chest.

"I don't *care* about all of that," I snap. "I don't care about anyone but Dorian!"

Ezra flinches.

I pause, mouth open, shocked at myself. I've harbored guilty thoughts like that before, said it to Dorian when he needed comfort, but I didn't mean to say it aloud. It was like something pushed the words out of me.

"I…I'm sorry, I didn't mean that," I whisper. "But please, Ezra…" I lean forward, taking one of his hands in mine.

There's a crackle of power as our fingers touch.

Ezra freezes. The color drains from his face.

I jerk back in my seat, suddenly afraid. "What?" I ask. "What did you just see?"

He looks away, his mouth opening and shutting as he struggles for words. Then he glances back at me, and his lips move, but no sound comes out, and—

* * *

I'm elsewhere. My head spins and my knees go weak, but strong arms hold me up. *Four* of them.

Dazed, I blink up at a familiar white mask above me. Nearby, static and distorted bits of song scream out of the radio as it rapidly switches. "Dorian?" I whisper.

I'm in his cell. I glance around, trying to reorient myself as my head spins. Is this real? A memory? My imagination?

Dorian's arms are solid as he holds me, but I pinch my own hand *hard*, just in case. A flare of pain tells me this is really happening, though I'm not sure how I got here.

152

Looking around again, I notice that the light on the camera is off. The shutters are closed, and so is the door. It's just Dorian and me in here, no Ezra, no MRF recording.

I don't know what just happened, but I must've convinced Ezra, somehow, to bring me here. I can't let the opportunity go to waste. I grab on to Dorian's shirt, but he pulls back like he's been burned. I finally get a good look at his eyes, wide and wild behind his mask. He looks…terrified.

"Dorian," I say, my voice trembling. All of me is trembling; there's a chill in my bones, a weird fog filling my thoughts. "We don't have much time. I need you to tell me the truth. *Please*." I reach for him, but when he flinches back, I grab at my own hair instead. Winding my fingers through the long strands in an attempt to hold myself together. "But I'm remembering. I know there was something else there that night."

The radio's song goes garbled. The lights flicker above us.

"No. *No!* No," the radio says, each one a different voice, a different volume.

"If you didn't do it, just tell me," I plead. "Then we can go home, Dorian. We can be together. Isn't that what you want?"

He retreats from me, fingers dragging down the sides of his mask hard enough that I can hear the awful scrape of it.

"What are you afraid of me remembering?" I ask, stepping closer to him. "There is nothing you could've done that would make me hate you. You're my best friend. My lover. My other half. Even if you did something awful, I know it was just to protect me. It's okay. Even if it was *me* who did it, please just tell me, I *promise* it'll be all right."

He looks up at me, his eyes haunted behind the mask. His mouth moves, and a moment later sound comes through the radio—his voice, whispering.

"Anything," he says. "I'd. Do. Anything. For you, Daisy."

"I know," I say with a sad smile. "So tell me the truth."

He takes a step closer to me. I stay very still, afraid to scare him off, as he slowly approaches.

"But you—" His voice in the radio gets louder, clearer, the closer he comes. "Betrayed me."

I jerk back. "What? No, I—"

"Turned me in to—" The radio switches to a mechanical voice, like an old recording. "Melsbach Research Facility."

"No," I croak. I can't remember, but I wouldn't have done that. I couldn't have. I refuse to believe it.

The radio goes back to Dorian's voice. "Abandoned me."

I step toward him despite my heart pounding in my ears. "But I came back! I was confused, I was scared, but I'm here now. I'm here for you, and I won't leave you again—"

"After I—" He steps closer too, until we are mere inches apart. "Killed. For you."

My heart drops. "What?"

"Killed. Your. Parents." His voice through the radio is clearer than it's ever been, but I can't seem to understand through the numbness. "For. *You.*"

"No," I say. "No, no, no, that can't be right…"

"You did this to me."

And suddenly his hands are around my neck, squeezing.

This isn't like the empty threat the last time I was here. He lifts me off the ground, grip cutting off my air entirely. His thumbs dig in until I gag. I struggle against him, choking and gasping for oxygen that won't come.

The door flies open behind me. My eyes dart toward it as my legs kick uselessly in the air. Ezra is there, striding toward us.

"That's enough," he says. "Get away from her, Dorian."

He flicks a handful of something at Dorian—*salt*—and Dorian flickers out of view.

I fall to my knees on the floor, gasping.

Dorian reappears, standing over me. He lets out a low animal snarl from behind his mask; the radio screeches and the lights flicker above us.

Even when Dorian had his hands on me, a part of me didn't believe he would truly hurt me. But Ezra…yes, I believe he would hurt Ezra.

"You," Dorian snarls through the radio.

He lunges toward Ezra, and I jut out a hand. "*Stop*," I shout, and the entire room seems to vibrate with the echo of my word. My emotions are a torrent, fear and regret and pain. I reach for my powers and they surge through me in answer.

Stronger than I expected.

Dorian *flies* across the room, his tall, spindly body slamming into the opposite wall. With a sharp *crack,* his mask splits down the middle. I gasp and drop my hand, cutting off the surge of power.

"Oh, God," I say. "Wait, I didn't mean—"

Dorian looks up at me, and I get a glimpse of twisted scar tissue and missing flesh before he covers his face and disappears from view.

Ezra, pale and trembling, turns to me. "Thank you," he whispers.

I stare wordlessly at the spot where Dorian disappeared. The shock in his expression keeps replaying in my mind.

For a few seconds, we are both frozen. Then someone clears their throat behind us. Ezra and I both turn to see a woman in a sharp suit standing in the open doorway, her expression one of barely contained fury.

"Mr. Bradford," she says, eyes narrowed on Ezra. "What exactly are you doing?"

Chapter Twenty-Two

"Dr. Wright." Ezra is frozen in place, his mouth opening and shutting multiple times as he struggles to find words. "I can explain."

"Go on, then," she says. "Explain to me why you appear to be running an undocumented, unapproved experiment in one of my labs over the weekend. Involving an outsider who I'm quite sure is not approved to be in a subject's room."

She's not looking at me, but I still feel the full weight of her judgment. Ezra's face colors.

"This is for one of my subjects," he says. "You don't understand—"

"You're right. I don't. Because you didn't give me a chance to understand it." Dr. Wright folds her arms over her chest, fixing him with a full glower. "Did you really think you could get away with this? That I wouldn't notice? I was willing to ignore to some of the discrepancies because I *trusted* you, and I thought you would come to me soon enough. But when I noticed that *someone else* used your keycard while you were in a meeting with me, *and* the cameras were shut off…" Dr. Wright finally glances at me. "Giving unauthorized access to a patient's room is beyond the bounds of what I consider acceptable, Ezra, no matter how much trust I've placed in you."

I go rigid. So does Ezra. But though he could easily blame the stolen keycard on me, he says nothing, his jaw set.

"Whatever this is, it's over now. If I can't trust you to handle your responsibility, then—"

"Dr. Wright—"

"It was me," I blurt. "I stole his keycard. He didn't know."

Dr. Wright turns to me. "And who exactly *are* you?"

"Gwen Bailey," I say. "I'm a ghost expert Ezra brought in for consultation." I clench my hands at my sides. I can't let Ezra take the fall for this. *Even if it means never seeing Dorian again?* a traitorous voice whispers in the back of my head, but I push it away. "He came here today to confront me because he realized I kept using his keycard to come here after hours. None of it was actually him."

Dr. Wright scowls at me, and then at Ezra. "Whether that's true or not, you're responsible for the people you bring into our facility," she says. "Consider yourself lucky that I'm not firing you on the spot. You disappoint me, Ezra."

* * *

I'm numb as the security guard takes my ID card. My shoulders are slumped, my eyes on my shoes. I can't even summon the energy to argue about it. What's the point? It's all over, anyway. It would've been over even if we hadn't been caught by Ezra's boss. Because Dorian will never be allowed to leave this place. He admitted that he killed my parents.

All I can think is: *Why?*

Dorian isn't a fool. He may be scattered and out of his mind sometimes, but not enough that he'd be oblivious to what his admission of guilt meant. Even if it's true, why admit it? The question plagues me as security escorts me off the premises of the MRF.

Ezra walks with me. "I have to come back to talk to Dr. Wright," he mutters as we go, not meeting my eyes. "But I'll drive you to your car first."

We spend the ride in silence. When we finally reach my car, still waiting in front of the house we fled a few hours ago, we both sit for several long moments.

"You should go somewhere safe," he says. "I'll come back and deal with the house after…whatever happens."

He still won't meet my eyes. When I reach for his hand, seeking reassurance, he flinches away.

I recoil, shocked.

"Ezra," I say. "I'm sorry."

"Don't be," he says, looking away. There's a hard set to his jaw that I've never seen before, and the tremble in his lower lip betrays him. I realize with a shock that he's crying. "You were right. Everything you said before. I'm just…a coward, through and through."

I stand frozen in shock. *I said that?* I had almost forgotten about the way I blacked out before I ended up in the cell with Dorian. I assumed I was acting like myself still, begging Ezra until he brought me to the MRF, but…

"I didn't mean that," I say, the excuse weak even to my own ears. "I wouldn't even be here without you."

"It's not enough." He covers his face, shoulders shaking. "I don't know if it'll ever be enough. I thought I could change things at the MRF if I did this right, but… Now I've failed Dorian like I've failed so many times before." He sucks in a shaky breath and lowers his hand, looking at me through reddened eyes. "Did you…get the answer you needed, at least?"

I stare at him—lost, helpless, defeated. I don't know what to say—how can I admit to him that we've been wrong this whole time? That Dorian is a killer and he will never be released as we hoped? So I say nothing.

He looks away. "Right," he murmurs.

"So it's over?" I ask, my voice quavering.

"You heard Dr. Wright. Maybe I can bring you in again, eventually. But…" He shrugs, looking lost.

Despair weighs on me. I know that won't happen. Even if I do get approved as a consultant again, it will mean no more secret late-night sessions, no more sneaking around with the cameras off. Being honest with Dr. Wright about the nature of our activities would involve both of us telling the MRF the truth about our powers, which would be an enormous risk. Even if Dr. Wright is sympathetic enough not to lock us up on the spot, we can't trust that it will be the same for all the higher-ups. But… "What about Dorian?" I ask. "We can't just leave him."

Ezra stares down at the steering wheel. "I'll continue to look after him as best as I can. Like I did before."

"But…" I shake my head, unable to form words. "But before, he was on the verge of disappearing. It's going to happen again, isn't it? Without me? You said it yourself. I'm his anchor to reality. Without me, it'll just go back to the way it was. Or worse."

"I'm sure I can arrange some visits," he says. "Like I said, I'll do the best I can, but…"

I stare at him. After all of this, he thinks I'll accept going back to the occasional visit? Probably through the glass again? No. I won't accept that. "You told me we were working toward freeing him," I say, frustration welling up in my tone.

"We were. But now that the MRF is aware of what we're doing, they'll… He…" Ezra throws out his hands in a helpless gesture. "We still don't know if it's safe to set him free, Daisy. I saw his hands around your neck. That conversation didn't go the way you hoped, did it?"

My lower lip trembles. I try to form an argument, but I'm not sure what to say. He's right: Dorian attacked us both. He confessed to the murders. I still believe we're missing something, but the evidence is stacking up against my old friend.

I don't even have my own memories to rely on.

Frustrated tears come to my eyes, and I blink them away. "So you're giving up on him."

Ezra's expression cracks. "No. Never. I'll see what I can do for him. But if he's going to be trapped forever, maybe it's kinder to let him pass on, Daisy."

I nod. But in my heart, I'm already steeling myself. I've lost Ezra, and I've lost Dorian, and any hope of the MRF's help.

I'm in this alone. Maybe I always have been.

Chapter Twenty-Three

I sit in the driver's seat of my car, gripping the steering wheel as I try to figure out what to do. The house is the last place I want to be right now, with the knowledge that something unseen is lurking in the shadows, but I have nowhere else to go. I have a growing headache and the weight of Dorian's confession on my shoulders, and I can barely think.

Why? I wonder again, still trying to wrap my mind around it. *Why would Dorian admit to the murders? Why damn himself? Why attack me?*

Unless...

I remember, abruptly, the way he flinched when I said he would do anything to protect me. No matter what, I still believe that was the truth. *Is* the truth. He'd do anything for me...including lying to protect me. Taking credit for a crime *I* committed. Pushing me away to keep me safe. I always knew that was a possibility.

I don't know why he would blame himself instead of whatever presence I've discovered in the house, but there must be a reason. There *must* be.

Am I being delusional? I don't know anymore. I can't trust myself or my own memories. Everything is such a confusing jumble in my head.

I don't know if there's a point anymore, if Dorian will ever be able to be free, but I still need to find out the truth. For myself, if nothing else. I *need* to know.

And I have one way to find it out.

* * *

The house seems bigger and emptier than ever when I walk in, but I know that's not true. There is something here. I stand in the foyer listening, *feeling*, trying to figure out where it is. But there's nothing but the usual soft creaks of the foundation.

"Are you hiding now?" I ask the darkness. Only silence answers me, but it doesn't matter. One way or another, I'm getting my answers.

When I explored my memories with Ezra's help, the attic was the one place that remained closed off to me. I expect that's where *that night* must be hiding from me in my own mind. It seems to be where the haunting is centered, too.

So I grab a hand mirror from my bedroom and head to the hatch in the upstairs hallway. There must be some connection, and I hope that being there physically will help me break down the wall sealing off my memory.

I fight back the surge of dread in my stomach as I pull the cord to lower the attic hatch. I climb up to the top of the ladder—and then stop, shocked, at the sight before me.

The last time I was up here, the attic was dusty but nearly empty aside from the record player. Now...

My eyes dart around, taking in the details one at a time. Half-melted candles are arranged in a half-circle. The corpse of a small bird lies bent and broken on the floor. Dried blood is smeared around it in the shape of a pentagram.

And in the middle of it all sits the record player—the center-piece of some kind of bloody *altar*.

I remember the other night, when time seemed to skip, and I woke with blood all over my hands. I assumed it was my own, but… Did *I* do this? Under the influence of whatever presence is in this house? Is the thing that killed Dorian now sinking its claws into me somehow?

My breath is coming hard and fast, creating small clouds in the air in front of me. It's devastatingly cold in here—which is one of the signs of a haunting Ezra mentioned, long ago.

I was right. Something is here. Something that *must* have played a part in whatever happened to my parents.

So though all of my instincts tell me to flee this place, I force myself to settle on the floor in a cross-legged position, clutching the mirror.

"I'm not afraid of you," I whisper.

I know this is a risk. My former journeys through my memories have proven that what happens in my mind can harm my body. I suspect that whatever I'm about to face will be more dangerous than anything else so far. But if this is what it takes to prove Dorian's innocence and understand what's happening to my mind and my body, I'll do it.

I hold the mirror in my lap and reach over to turn on the record player. "Daisy Bell" begins to play its bittersweet, familiar tune.

Without Ezra and the metronome to guide me, I have to find my own path into my mind and out of it. I will have to rely on the familiar sound of the record player to lead me back to safety after I find what I need in my memories.

I stare into the eyes of my reflection.

"This is my mind," I remind myself. "These are my memories. I am in charge, and nothing is hidden from me that I cannot choose to uncover."

As I slowly shut my eyes and let my head fall forward, I can almost hear the echo of the metronome in my mind. *Tick, tick, tick, tick...*

* * *

I open my eyes, and I am in the endless hallway of my memories again. As I walk, doors creak open on either side. I catch a glimpse of Dorian taking off his own head and juggling it for me while the child version of me claps in glee. Behind another door, our young adult selves kiss in the bathtub. In another, I am weeping in my closet while Dorian stands over me, hunched protectively, his gloved hands covering my ears.

I refuse to be distracted by any of them. My eyes stay on the attic hatch. It isn't rattling today, like the thing on the other side understands that I am coming for it. Like it's waiting for me.

"I'm not afraid of you," I whisper, and grab the cord. I pull—

It catches. Resisting.

I shut my eyes, grit my teeth. "This is *my* mind," I say. I yank again, and the hatch opens an inch, revealing a sliver of darkness—but it catches on a chain lock. Something is trying to keep me out. "You can't hide my own memories from me," I mutter, pushing all of my concentration into opening it again. The chain rattles and slides—slowly but surely—until there's a click.

The hatch creaks open.

For a second, I wonder what, exactly, is working so hard to keep me away. If this is my own mind, then am I fighting against *myself*? Did *I* lock this away so tightly? But I have only a moment to wonder, because the hatch is open and the ladder is waiting. There's nothing left to do but climb into the darkness and relive the night I forced myself to forget.

** * **

Tick, tick, tick.

The dinner table is silent enough to hear the clock's movement and the soft scrape of utensils across plates. I push my food around, my stomach too knotted to eat. When I fumble and accidentally drop my knife, the clang of it against the floorboard rings out like a gunshot.

I flinch. My mother flinches too and then glares. My father does not look up from his meal, but his lips press into a thin line.

I lean over. When I lift the tablecloth, Dorian peers up from beneath it, holding out the fallen knife in one hand. A show of solidarity; he knows how I hate these family dinners. I don't dare speak to him in front of my parents—I've made that error plenty of times when I was younger—but a smile curves the corner of my lips as I sit up again with the utensil in hand.

"Is something funny?" my father asks. His tone is enough to make the bruises on my wrists ache anew.

But they're hidden beneath my sleeves. Beneath the façade of a perfect daughter and a perfect family.

I glance at him, but he still seems focused on his meal. And emptying his glass of whiskey. "No, Father. May I be excused?"

"You've hardly touched your food," my mother says, tutting under her breath.

"Go on," my father says.

"But Pat—"

"I've made my decision, Nina." His voice is suddenly loud, cracking like a whip.

My mother and I both tense. She glares at me across the table. She'll blame me, later, for what happens after he's had a few more drinks. My heartbeat rises with the realization, and the lights flicker.

My mother looks up at them and back at me. My father continues drinking his whiskey. Nobody says anything; we are all very good at pretending that everything is fine and normal in this house.

I walk to the kitchen, emptying the remnants of my meal into the trash before rinsing my plate. The hiss of voices from the other room is audible above the rush of water.

"—caught her talking to herself in her room again," my mother says. "It's getting out of hand."

"Something wrong with her. Always has been."

I look up at Dorian, who is sitting on the counter beside the sink, long legs dangling. He shrugs at me, a silent question: *are you okay?*

I shrug back, a silent answer: *it's nothing new.* But I go still at the next snippet of my father's words. I pause, water running over my hands, straining to listen without making it obvious.

"…Send her away somewhere…"

"But what will people say?" My mother's voice grows shriller. "Our daughter in a mental hospital? We'll be the talk of the town!"

"We already are!" my father thunders. He's getting loud now, his words slurring, no longer attempting to prevent me from overhearing. "You hear what they say. Crazy Daisy, they call her."

My stomach plummets. The lights flicker overhead once, twice. The conversation in the other room goes silent.

My power is a livewire beneath my skin, itching for escape. It's been getting worse lately, harder to control. Sometimes I catch my parents glancing at me with fear in their eyes. Sometimes I think they're right to be afraid.

I shut off the water and walk toward the stairs before they can start up again, or worse, call me in. The conversation, this time, is an exchange of heated whispers. My heart is pounding. What will happen if they send me away? If I lose Dorian? I can't imagine it. He's the only thing that holds me together. And without me, it will just be my parents in the house. Dorian will be stuck with them and—

I pause, bottom step creaking beneath my foot, as music sputters to life above me. My eyes flicker up to the hallway, where I hear the thump of the attic ladder coming down. The song "Run, Rabbit, Run!" spills from the space above, and my blood goes cold.

He's here. I didn't even think his name this time. He's getting stronger.

In a blink, Dorian is in front of me, taking my hand between two of his gloved ones. Another presses over my eyes.

I shut them and let him lead me blindly up the stairwell. When he presses me against the wall in the hallway, I go still, eyes closed. I can hear the song playing and the sound of my parents arguing below, growing progressively louder though the words have become indecipherable. But louder than either is the thump of footsteps in the hallway, just a few feet away from me.

I clutch at Dorian. He's trembling. We hold each other close as the footsteps approach. They pause beside us—and then continue onward, downward, creaking along the steps I just climbed. Dorian tugs on my hand and we head to my room. I drop to my knees and climb under the bed, and Dorian is close behind. He holds me, two arms wrapped around my waist, the other two covering my ears to block out the growing sound of my parents' shouting.

"Where are you going?" I hear my mother shriek. "Don't walk away from me—"

My parents can't see the thing that lives in the attic, but they *feel* him, whether they know it or not. Just like he feels their fear, their anger. He stokes the flames and feeds off the ensuing chaos. A vicious cycle. All I can do is block it out as best as I can. Whenever I look at him, give him my attention, even *think* about him, it only makes him stronger.

And he's been growing very strong lately. I've been trying to find a way out, for both me and for Dorian, but our attempts to get him to cross the property line have proved futile, and I can't leave him behind.

When Dorian removes his hands from my ears, the house is silent. Weirdly silent. My parents are no longer screaming in the dining room. The record player is no longer playing *his* song, but skipping, over and over again, the song deep and distorted.

"Run- Run- Run- Run-"

"What—" I start to ask, but Dorian places a finger to my lips. His eyes are wide behind the mask, shifting toward the doorway to my room.

The stairs creak. Then there's another sound—a dragging, scraping sound of something being pulled across the floorboards. As it gets closer, I hear, too, the sound of footsteps. The heavy thuds of my father's shoes.

Step, scrape.

Step, scrape.

Step.

Right outside my bedroom door. I hold my breath, my hands fisted in Dorian's shirt. He is silent, tense beside me.

"Daisy," my father says. It's his stern voice, the one that means I'm in trouble.

Step, scrape.

He's inside my bedroom.

"Daisy, come out now," my father says. "Stop acting like a child."

I inch that way out of instinct; punishment is always worse if I disobey. But Dorian grabs me and holds me close, keeping me under the bed. His body trembles against my back. He presses a gloved finger to my lips.

Step. My father's shoes come into view from my vantage point under the bed. Polished and glossy black.

Scraaape.

He drags an axe across the floor behind him. Its blade is rusty—and dripping with fresh blood.

The song upstairs cuts off abruptly, leaving behind a terrible silence.

Dorian's hand stifles my gasp. But then he slowly releases me. I reach for him as he pulls away, but he shakes his head and disappears from view.

I stay there, trembling, heart pounding in my ears.

"Little rabbit..." my father whispers, but it doesn't sound like his voice at all. It's too deep, too old, too inhuman.

I jump at a sudden *thump* from behind my closed closet door. But as the thing inside my father moves that way, I realize it must be Dorian causing a distraction for me. I crawl to the edge of the bed and wait one second, two, until I hear the creak of the closet door opening and the sound of my father shuffling around in search of me. Then I roll out from under the bed, lurch to my feet, and race out the door.

My bare feet pound against the floorboards as I head to the stairs.

I lurch to a stop at the top of the staircase, hand flying to my mouth. My mother is facedown at the bottom of the steps, hair spread around her, one hand outstretched. Her back is a mess of gore and gristle where the axe came down. She must have been crawling away—to me, or the front door, I'll never know.

I swallow my scream as I hear footsteps thumping out of my bedroom behind me. I stumble down the stairs and force myself to step over my mother's body. Tears blur my vision as I run for the front door. I grab the handle, pull it open—but as I step forward, a hand grabs me by the hair and yanks me back. My feet slip in my mother's blood, and the thing inside of my father slams the door shut and locks it with his free hand.

"Going somewhere?" he whispers, and I look up into a pair of eyes that burn red as he reaches to pick up the axe again.

Chapter Twenty-Four

Iscrabble at the hand holding my hair, but my struggles are in vain. My powers don't answer when I call, either; I'm too scared. They have always come to me in moments of anger or concentration, and I can find neither when I am drowning in the sound of my own heartbeat.

Suddenly, Dorian is there. He appears, visible and solid, pushing between us. He has always been the bigger one, the faster one, the braver of the two of us. I hit the floor and scramble backward, gasping for breath.

The thing possessing my father tilts his head, looking at Dorian.

"Leave her alone," Dorian says, "Dad."

My father's red eyes narrow even as he grins. "Was wondering when you'd have the guts to show yourself, boy." He takes a step closer, radiating menace, but Dorian holds his ground even as he shakes.

I remember Dorian whispering to me the first night he crawled out from under my bed, when I held his bloodied hands and asked what happened to him.

"My dad," he whispered. "He killed my mama. When I found

her body in the attic, he killed me too."

Dorian got his revenge, eventually—whispering into his father's ear every time he tried to sleep till the awful man put a gun in his mouth. But that only trapped him here with Dorian. And he's been getting stronger—growing until he twisted into something else, something even more evil than he was in life.

"Didn't I teach you this lesson already, boy?" he snarls, and swings the axe at Dorian.

I expect it to go straight through him. So, I think, does Dorian. But instead, it strikes him right in the mask, splitting it down the middle.

The broken pieces clatter to the floorboards. Dorian stumbles back, covering his face with both hands. With each step back, he grows smaller, until his back hits the wall and he's in the form of the child he was when we first met. Just a thin, cowering boy, his fingertips raw and bloody from when he was dragged out from under the bed by the same man he's now facing. His face a mess of gore and bone. Terrified and alone.

But no. Not alone. Because I am still here, and the sight of my friend reduced to such a state reawakens the anger I've been searching for.

"Leave him alone!" I scream, rising to my feet. Dorian has defended me so many times. Protected me, comforted me, reassured me. Now it's my turn.

The monster in my father's body laughs, an awful, grating sound.

"What are you going to do, little rabbit?" he asks.

In response, I jut out a hand and *push*. He slides back on the floorboards, face shifting into an almost comical mask of surprise. It takes only a second to recover, though. He raises the axe and lunges. I push with my mind again, and he jerks to a stop—but then slowly, as if moving against a current, he takes a step forward. And another. Each grows easier, more confident. And he's moving not toward me, but toward the cowering form of Dorian, still curled into a ball in the corner.

"Dorian," I force out, struggling to regain my hold. "Run!"

Instead of disappearing, Dorian peeks at me through his fingers. "Go," he mouths, and I realize it isn't fear that's keeping him rooted and vulnerable. He's trying, as always, to protect me.

"No!" I could run for the door but can't bear to leave Dorian behind. I can't lose him. No matter what it takes, I *have* to save him.

I shut my eyes, curl my fingers, and *scream* as I push at the thing possessing my father with all of the energy I have.

I hear a horrible, wet squelch. The thump of a body hitting the floor.

I fall to my knees on the floorboards, gasping, my vision going white. But I force myself to lift my head and look to see if Dorian— If Dorian is—

Fine. He's fine.

And my father's body is slumped on the floor just a foot from him, with the blade of the axe buried deeply in his face. Splitting it directly down the middle, just like what was done to Dorian so long ago.

A sob wrenches out of my throat as I crawl forward on my hands and knees. "Dad…" I whisper, voice shaking. I reach for the body, but then I recoil and turn instead to Dorian. He's growing already, changing until he's an adult again. Without the mask, his face is still a mess of scar tissue, cheekbone caved in and most of his nose destroyed.

I pull his hands away from his face and kiss him.

"You saved me," I whisper.

"You saved *me*," he murmurs back, his forehead pressing against mine.

"Dorian, what are we going to do?" I ask. "My parents…" My voice wobbles. I feel numb, ears ringing, unable to wrap my mind around this. I can't stop shaking. "I have to call the police. But what if they take me away? From this house, from you? I'll—"

I cut off as I hear something upstairs. The scratch of the record player…and a jaunty, familiar tune beginning to play again.

My eyes widen. I pull back from Dorian, see an answering fear in his eyes. I open my mouth to voice a question—

But suddenly I can't speak. Can't move. Cold fingers wrap around my neck from behind, chilly breath ghosting against my ear. When I glance sideways, a pair of red eyes and a horrible, leering grin await.

"Godric Elwood," he mouths, but it's my lips that speak the word. His name.

And then my body turns and looks at Dorian. I am a passenger in my own mind. It's like I'm viewing the world from within a cage. I can even feel the cold bars against my hands, rattle them mentally, but I am helpless to do anything but watch as my body reaches out and grabs Dorian by the throat. He struggles against my grip, but he doesn't fight. He *won't* fight me.

"Dorian," I scream within the confines of my head. I hear Godric's laughter echoing around me. I can *see* him through the bars of this cage, even as I simultaneously view myself choking Dorian. A disconcerting double vision, my mind and body torn apart.

In my mindscape, Godric is red and wet like flayed-open

muscle, his eyes twin flames, horns curling out of his head. Once a horrible man, now become even something worse in death.

"I've been waiting so long for this," he hisses. "Waiting, feeding… But such *power*. It was worth the wait. Your mind is a weapon. And your body…" His forked tongue slides out from behind his blackened lips.

One of my hands is still gripping Dorian by the throat, holding him with preternatural strength. The other slides down over my body, my breasts. I can *feel* it, the horrifying sensation of being violated by my own hand. Nobody but Dorian has touched me so intimately. I never wanted anyone else to.

I scream and thrash against the bars of my own mind. Dorian's eyes are rolling back in his head. His form flickers around the edges. *Can he die again?*

"There are worse things than death," Godric says, answering the question I only asked in my mind. "I can send him down to the pits of hell, a new plaything for my master."

Nothing is mine anymore. Not my body, my thoughts, my Dorian, my power…

My power.

I am not helpless. I have control of *my* power. I reach for it buried inside of me, let it wrap around me like a comforting cloak, along with my anger. How *dare* this entity use my body like this. I am not a tool or a weapon or a thing. I picture the cage around me again, and then I picture the door opening and me striding out.

I let go of Dorian's throat. My hand remains in the air, trembling as I battle for control.

Dorian has done his best to protect me. Now it's my turn to return the favor. I raise my trembling, resisting hands to my temples and screw my eyes shut as I concentrate.

"Get *out*," I say through gritted teeth.

The creature howls in response. He digs his claws into me mentally, resisting me as I try to shove him away. Warm blood trickles from my nose, cascading over my lips and chin, but I ignore it.

"This is my body," I whisper. "My mind. You can't have it."

Another gush of blood from my nose, and pain racks me. I crumble to my knees. But warm hands are there to catch me before I hit the floor. Dorian's long arms wrap around me, and he presses his unmasked forehead to mine in a show of silent support. He's weak and flickering, but he's here, lending me strength. My other half. Power pulses through me—power that I loaned him every time I spoke with him, laughed with him, shaped him. Now it flows back into me, helping me fight.

The monster is still snarling and clawing at me, trying to break free. It's agony to try to force him out of my head, but I realize, all of a sudden, that I don't have to.

I can do something better.

I picture the cage again, the one he locked me in. But I build it stronger this time. Not a cage but a room with four sturdy walls. Somewhere out of the way, where he can rage all he wants and no one will hear. Somewhere like-

The attic.

I picture myself standing in front of the monster as he struggles and snarls, held in place by the combined power of me and Dorian. Then I place my hands on his chest and *shove*. He stumbles, tries to recover, and all four of Dorian's hands appear from behind me to shove as well, forcing the creature into the room.

I shut the hatch, slam a mental lock into place, and suddenly my head is quiet. I'm alone in my body, sagging on the floor in Dorian's arms.

"We did it," I whisper, leaning against him. But he doesn't feel as solid as before. He's still fuzzy around the edges, his form indistinct. I raise my head, blinking, confusion soon sharpening into fear. "Dorian? What's wrong?" I grab hold of his arms, forcibly anchoring him as his form flickers. "Oh, no. What did I do?" He gave me my power back to help me fight. And I…

I blink, disoriented, as the memory slips through my fingers. What did I do? I shake my head to clear it, and the world spins. I reach for Dorian, but my hand goes through him, and he disappears. It's just me, alone with the bodies of my parents, blood dripping from my nose, memories bleeding away…

* * *

The scene freezes like a movie being paused. But my eyes can still move, flickering around the room. Blood still seeps from my nose, a drip growing into a stream, forming a puddle on the floorboards where Dorian used to be.

Bubbles form, and then a hand reaches out, coated in the viscous red liquid. Long nails dig into the floorboards, and a figure slowly drags itself out of the blood, inch by inch, and stands over me.

Red and grinning and horned. *Godric.*

He wipes blood off his face and turns burning eyes on me. He grins, a mouthful of sharp white teeth emerging from beneath the blood still dripping from its skin.

"Yes, that's how it happened," he says. "You locked me away. Me and every memory that I appeared in." He takes a step toward me, gait awkward and shuffling, like he's still remembering how. "But now you've opened the door."

I'm paralyzed as memories slam into me. I remember that night, and I remember that it's been years since then. My body isn't really here; it's sitting in the attic.

I shut my eyes. "Wake up, wake up…" I tell myself. I try to hear the song on the record player so I can follow it back to reality, but there's nothing but Godric's echoing laughter.

"Just you and me now, little rabbit," he snarls. He grabs me by the chin and my eyes fly open. He leans down to drag one claw down my cheek, leaving a line of burning pain. I scream and try to pull away, but I can't.

I'm trapped in my own mind with him.

That hatch rattling in the hallway of my memories…it was never just a bad memory trapped on the other side. It was this *thing* that I forced myself to forget. I've had him locked away all this time.

And that's why Dorian said it was dangerous to remember. The more time I spent with him, the more I recalled my lost memories, the more the cage I had placed around Godric weakened. But in the end, it didn't matter. I released him myself.

He grips my chin between his pointer and thumb. Claws dig into my skin, and his hot, rank breath ghosts over my face. This is real. He can really hurt me. I already knew that from exploring my mind with Ezra, but now I'm trapped here.

"All these years I've spent locked away," he whispers. "And I…am so…*hungry.*" A long tongue flicks out of his mouth and rakes over the tears trickling down my face.

"Those nights in my house," I whisper. The song. The sounds in the night. The incident in my bathtub. I thought I was going crazy, or my abilities were going haywire, but I was wrong all along. "That was you."

"Every time you unlocked a memory, the door cracked open a little further," he says. "I wanted to speed things along. Jolt your memory." He grips my face hard. "And I couldn't resist taking your body on a couple of test rides."

I shut my eyes, trying in vain to turn away, but his grip holds me steady. All this time, and Dorian knew. *That's* why he tried to push me away, to stop me. He knew the danger of remembering. He was willing to be forgotten if it kept me safe. And I didn't listen.

"He can't help you this time," Godric says, hearing my thoughts. He leans closer, nose brushing my cheek, smearing blood over my skin. "It's just you and me now, Daisy. I may be locked up in your mind, but now you're here with me. We're going to have so much fun together…"

"Daisy!"

The voice is familiar but so far away, so very far. But Godric pauses, glancing around like he's trying to find the source.

"Ezra!" I scream. "Help me!"

Godric chuckles. "He can't hear you. Not here."

He's probably right. But it doesn't matter, because I can hear him. I shut my eyes, using Ezra's voice as a lifeline, an anchor back to reality, like I did so many times in the MRF.

"Listen to the sound of my voice."

"What is this?" Godric hisses.

"Let it guide you back to your body."

"No. Stop that. You're mine. You're trapped here with me!" His voice is growing frantic. His claws rake my cheek, slashing deep into my skin, but the pain feels distant now—and Ezra's voice sounds closer.

This isn't real. *That* is reality.

"On the count of three, you're going to open your eyes and wake up."

"No!" Godric howls.

"One… two… *three.*"

I open my eyes.

Chapter Twenty-Five

I gasp awake, pulling air into my starved lungs. Terror still grips me, making my chest tight and my heart pound. My cheek burns where Godric's claws raked my skin. But I am *awake*. I am *out*. I escaped the prison of my own mind. This is real, and I am here in the attic. I clutch the mirror to ground myself, gripping it so hard that it hurts. The pain is almost comforting. I look at my own reflection, see the bleeding gashes over my cheekbone.

"Ezra." My voice trembles. He's kneeling in front of me in the pentagram, his head lowered. "We had it all wrong. It wasn't me or Dorian that killed my parents. And it wasn't my house that's haunted. It's me, it's been me this whole time, he's been inside of my head *this whole time...*"

I look up and my breath catches. Ezra is staring at me, unblinking, head cocked at an unnatural angle. Blood drips from one nostril, spills over his lips and down his chin to splatter on the floorboards, and he doesn't react.

For a heart-stopping moment, I think he's dead. Then his mouth moves.

"Daisy," he says, and it's not Ezra's voice. It's not Ezra.

The horrible realization seeps into me. I remember the words spelled out on the Ouija board when I asked Godric what he wanted: *LET ME OUT*. This whole time, I assumed he was trapped in the house, but I was wrong. He was trapped in my head. And I just opened the door for him.

The monster that murdered Dorian and my parents is free, and it's all my fault.

Fresh terror spreads ice through my body, making it hard to breathe again. "Godric," I say. "Let him go."

A smile spreads across his face and keeps spreading until it looks painful. It's too wide, too toothy, entirely unsuited to Ezra's face. "Oh? Is this your friend?" He twitches, neck jerking into an even deeper angle. "Yes. I see. I just thought about killing you, and he screamed quite loudly."

My lower lip trembles. *Ezra is still in there.* I remember what it felt like to have Godric take control of me, to feel helpless behind my own eyes. "Let him go," I say again. "It's me you want."

"But you locked me up." He looks at his hands, flexing his fingers; they stay frozen in stiff, unnatural positions, like he isn't quite sure what to do with them. "This one is more accommodating. More…pliable."

"You can't have him."

"Why not? What are you so afraid of?" He grins that sickening grin at me again. "This, maybe?"

He grabs the mirror from my hands and bashes his face into it. Once, twice, leaving a smear of blood behind. I scream, lurching forward to stop him from hurting himself, from hurting Ezra. The thing in his body is laughing, fresh blood spurting from his nose. The lights flicker.

He raises a hand and an invisible force shoves me backward. I fly back, slamming into the wall, hard. Then I'm on the floor, tasting blood.

I can only lie there, ears ringing, the flickering lightbulb casting everything in a nightmarish haze. I'm frozen as Ezra's body stands and steps over me and toward the ladder.

Free. Because of me.

When he's gone, I struggle to my feet, breath shaky.

He's out. I let him out. What will he do with a body like Ezra's, *power* like Ezra's?

I'm struck by the urge to run. To get as far away from here as possible before everything falls apart.

But I'm not leaving Dorian again. Before I decide anything else, I have to go get my own monster. Yet I have an uneasy feeling that Godric may be headed to the same place.

* * *

I lean over the wheel and race through the dark streets, praying it's not too late. Luckily, the roads are empty at this time of night. Ash Valley is dark and quiet except for the sole building still lit up on the edge of town. The Melsbach Research Facility.

When something slams into my windshield, I scream and slam on the brakes. The car screeches to a stop. My headlights pierce the darkness of an empty road. It happened too quickly for me to see what hit me, but judging by the smear of blood and feathers it left behind, I have a suspicion.

Then a second magpie dives out of the night and smashes into my windshield. I scream again, instinctively covering my face. A third is soon behind, this one hitting my driver's side window. I stay still, hands clasped to my ears and eyes shut, until I'm sure that nothing more is coming. Then I silently recite the rhyme in my head, and my stomach drops.

One for sorrow,
Two for joy,
Three for a girl,
Four for a boy,
Five for silver,
Six for gold,
Seven for a secret never to be told.
Eleven for health.
Twelve for wealth.
Thirteen, beware!

"*It's the devil himself,*" I whisper, and raise my shaking hands to grip the wheel.

"*Spirits can warp over time, become something that most of us would call a demon,*" Ezra once said.

"*I can send him down to the pits of hell, a new plaything for my master,*" Godric told me.

He was always a monster, but now he's something worse.

I consider driving home or out into the desert, leaving Ash Valley behind forever. But then I think of Dorian sitting in that cell, waiting for me. Trying to push me away to protect me. Willing to fade from existence if it meant I was safe.

I can't leave him. Not this time. No matter the risk. I wipe my eyes, steel myself, and press on the gas, racing toward the MRF and the monster that killed my parents.

Chapter Twenty-Six

When I pull up to the gate to the MRF, the lights flicker and die. *All* of them. The facility is usually a beacon on the edge of the late-night town, but now it is as dark and dead quiet as the rest of Ash Valley.

The guard station is empty, the gate to the facility parking lot left wide open. Dread is a cold knot in my stomach as I drive through, and I'm not surprised to see that Ezra's car is already here, parked haphazardly in front of the entrance.

I slam the car door and rush into the empty, dark lobby. I flash my cell phone around the room, but there's nothing here but a smear of blood across the tile. The door that leads to the holding cells has been blown off its hinges, leaving a hole like a gaping maw. Beyond is a hallway lit only by dim red emergency lights.

My gut urges me to run for the exit without looking back. Instead, I slide along the wall. The silence and darkness in this building are thick, suffocating. The sound of my own breathing seems to echo. I'm scared to use my cell phone and attract attention, so I feel my way through and count the cells as I pass them.

Thirteen...fourteen...fifteen. This should be Dorian's room. I grab the handle, but it's locked.

I pause to breathe. I was hoping the power shutdown would have released him, but there must be a backup generator providing the emergency lighting and security. When I look over my shoulder, the light on the hallway camera is still blinking, too.

I'm cut off from Dorian. Fear is a living thing wrapped around me, constricting my throat and my chest. It makes it hard to breathe, hard to think. But I dig past it and reach for what it's kept buried for far too long: my anger.

All my life I have pushed that anger down for the sake of staying in control. Of maintaining appearances. Of keeping myself small and unnoticed. But now, I let myself feel it. The years of running, of loneliness. The unfairness of how everything has been ripped away from me. I have been forced to be small for far too long. I have forced myself to be submissive and docile in the name of being safe.

Not this time. Never again.

If I use my powers here, in the middle of the MRF, the camera will record it. They will know I'm exactly the kind of monster they keep locked within these walls. I may never be able to conceal myself again…

But if that's what it takes to save Dorian, then so be it. I am tired of hiding from what I really am.

I press my hands against the cell door and let my anger fill me. First it's a trickle clawing up the back of my throat. Then the dam breaks and the anger pours out until it fills me to the brim and overflows in a scream. I scream until my throat is raw, and my body is shaking, and the door in front of me is rattling with the force of my fury and my *power*.

And I let it out.

Metal shrieks as the door dents and warps. I scream again, shoving my palms against the iron. This time it flies off its hinges, slamming backward and into the secondary door trapping Dorian. It blows right through it, and both hit the wall inside Dorian's cell, leaving the room open.

I step through the doorway, panting. I instinctively wipe my nose, but there's no blood. That was always Godric bashing against the inside of his cell. My own power doesn't hurt me.

"Dorian?" I ask, my voice barely a whisper, hoarse in the aftermath of that scream. It wasn't until this moment that I realized I'm going to have to tell him everything—that I ignored his warnings, that I released his father just like he feared I would.

Dorian was willing to lose me to keep Godric trapped. What if he hates me for what I've done?

A tear rolls down my cheek—and Dorian blinks into existence in front of me, lit by the red emergency lights, wiping it away with one gloved thumb. His fingers lightly graze the scratch marks his father left on my cheek. I stare up at him. His mask is still cracked down the middle, revealing a sliver of scars, the evidence of what his father did to him when he was just a child. My throat is so tight with guilt that I can't force out any words. But he pulls me against him as if he already knows.

"I'm so sorry," I whisper, my face muffled where it presses against Dorian's chest. "You were just trying to protect me. But I didn't listen."

Dorian strokes my hair with one gloved hand, the other three holding me safe against him. The radio is silent behind him, likely dead from the power outage.

I pull back enough to look up at him, blinking away my tears. "I let him out, Dorian. He took Ezra's body. He's free now, and he's *here*, and it's all my fault."

His eyes widen in panic, and he nudges me toward the door.

"I'm not leaving without you," I say. I step back, tugging his hand. He follows, step by step, but stops as I step over the doorway. "What's wrong?"

He looks at the open doorway and then past it, into the hallway. He looks at me, a terrible sadness in his eyes, and shakes his head.

"What do you mean, you can't? I've remembered everything, your father is out, we can be together now…" I trail off, realizing he's still looking at me with those sad, sad eyes. He points at the walls, the floor, the ceiling, gesturing all around him with all four hands.

"You're still trapped," I whisper. Of course it wasn't the doors keeping Dorian in; he's incorporeal most of the time. I never figured out how they moved Dorian from my house to this place, but somehow this entire cell must be built to contain him. "But…no. No, this can't be. I…" I suck in a shaky breath, trying to make sense of it. This can't end with me walking away again. We're supposed to be together. I did *all* of this so we could be together.

"No," I say again. "Not now. Not when we're so close." Tears build behind my eyes, and I struggle to keep myself from breaking down. This is our chance to get out of here. "I'm not leaving you behind again."

Dorian takes a step back, away from me, his image starting to fade.

I shake my head, unable to speak through the tears thickening my throat. It's not fair. I can't come this far, get this close to being with Dorian, only to have it ripped away like this.

"I don't want to live without you," I say. "Because I'm yours, and you're mine. Forever, remember? That's the way it's supposed to be."

Memories flicker through my mind. Our childlike laughter as we ran through the halls of my house. Nights spent curled around each other in bed. Our kiss in this very cell. When I thought he disappeared, and I brought him back…

My rushing thoughts halt.

"Ezra said that iron and salt trap ghosts," I say, thinking as I speak. "Maybe that's what's keeping you here. But Dorian…" I step forward into the cell, reach out, and take two of his gloved hands in mine. "You're not a ghost." I press my lips to one glove and look up at him, into his dark eyes behind the mask. "You're my imaginary friend." I smile through my tears. "Which means you are what I make you."

Ezra has always said that I shaped Dorian, changed him. That he doesn't act like any other ghost that Ezra has seen in his years of study.

Maybe he was a poltergeist when I found him, but now he's something different. Something more powerful.

Something that isn't restricted by whatever rules bind him here, because I *believe* he isn't.

I hold that thought in my mind, pouring every ounce of myself into it. Pouring my power into Dorian, willing him to *change*, like he's changed so many times for me. When I gave him the mask, when I grew up and wanted him to grow with me, when he grew extra appendages just to please me. When he stopped existing and I summoned him back.

Still holding his hands, I step backward, pulling him with me. And then another. When he stalls, I give an insistent tug. His hands tense as they move toward the barrier as if fearing pain—but still trusting me.

His hands move into the doorway and through it.

CHAPTER TWENTY-SIX

And Dorian steps into the hallway with me, free of his cell.

191

Chapter Twenty-Seven

Dorian is finally free, and we are finally together, as we were always supposed to be. But stepping into the dark hallway reminds me that he's not the only monster loose in this facility, and we're not safe yet.

Dorian cups my face with his gloved hand, tilting my chin up so I look at him. I watch as the crack in his mask seals together until it's whole once more. "What now, my darling?"

I startle. He's *speaking* without the radio. He still *sounds* like a radio, his voice faintly staticky and musical, but the words and the voice are all his own. I've freed him in more ways than one, it seems.

But my smile fades as I consider his question.

What next, indeed. It would be easy for us to slip out amid the chaos. Now that Dorian is free, we could leave the MRF and Ash Valley behind and start a new life together, just the two of us. That would be safest, now that I've revealed myself to their security cameras.

I could run away again, leaving behind the monster that I set free and all of the destruction he'll cause. I can abandon Ezra like I once abandoned Dorian.

I shake my head before the thought is fully formed. "We can't leave," I say. Then I correct, "*I* can't leave. You can. You should. Go while you can. You can go to the house and wait for me there, or…or go wherever you want." I've finally set him free, like he should've been all this time. Free even from me. "You don't need me anymore."

But Dorian huffs a laugh from behind his mask. "You think I'll leave you now?" His grip on my chin tightens, and he shakes me playfully. "Never again, Daisy."

"But I don't know what's going to happen," I say. "Even if I can banish that thing once and for all, you might end up locked in a cell again. And if I can't beat Godric, then…" Then I'll die trying. Even that will be better than running and living with the guilt.

"We will never be parted again," Dorian says. "Not even by death. I swear it."

The idea of dying together shouldn't be romantic. But…he's right. It's *right* for us to be together, forever and always.

"Do you think we can fight your father?" I ask. "Together?"

"I think we can do anything together," Dorian says. "Believe it, and I'll make it so."

From anyone else, that would be a hollow promise. But from Dorian, I know it's true. Dorian is my imaginary friend. He's been shaped—and limited—by my beliefs all of this time. But now I understand the power of our bond. The power inside of *me*. And I refuse to bottle it up and pretend it doesn't exist ever again.

I press up on my tiptoes and carefully lift Dorian's mask just enough kiss him. When I pull back, I whisper, "I believe you can do anything."

I catch a glimpse of a smile—his real smile—before the mask slots back into place, hiding him behind that ferocious forever-grin. "Then what will you have me do?"

"Get that thing out of Ezra and send him back to hell where he belongs." I squeeze his hands. "*Without* hurting Ezra. Please. He's my friend."

Dorian hesitates. But when he sees the plea in my expression, he inclines his long body in a deep bow. "As you say, darling."

Together, we go to face my demon.

Chapter Twenty-Eight

I t's easy to find Ezra. All we have to do is follow the trail of bodies.

Security guards lie in contorted positions in the hallways of the MRF, limbs bent in impossible positions, spines and necks broken, eyes frozen wide open.

One of them is still alive—barely. He's clawing at his own face, whimpering, leaving bloody rivets in his own skin. I crouch down beside him, touching a finger to his forehead.

"Sleep," I whisper, and he goes limp.

I sigh, straightening. Thank God only the skeleton night shift crew was here, or the damage could've been much worse. Still, it is terrible. And a terrifying amount of power.

Dorian is a comforting presence beside me, his gloved fingers brushing against mine as we walk. With each touch, power zaps through my body. With my memories back and him at my side, I'm at my full potential…but will it be enough?

I have no idea what Godric is capable of with Ezra's body. And if I win by locking the demon away in my mind like last time, I will lose Dorian all over again. I won't do that.

One way or another, Dorian and I will end this together, as it always should've been.

I feel Ezra's presence before I see him. Power radiates off him, an invisible miasma that leaves my skin prickling with unease. All of my senses scream to run, but I refuse. *Not this time.* I force myself to keep moving, even though terror thickens the air. It crawls over me like the legs of a thousand bugs scritch-scratching at my skin. I taste copper on the back of my tongue and hear the drum of my heartbeat in my ears.

Then I round the corner and he's there.

Ezra stands with his head tilted at an odd angle, his fingers rigid and contorted at his sides. He is covered in blood from head to toe, and when he turns at the sound of our footsteps, his eyes are black. He grins, and it's horrible, lips stretching until it looks painful, every tooth on display. There's blood on them, too.

"Daisy," he says, and it's not Ezra's voice at all. It's Godric, and it makes every hair on my body stand at attention. The red emergency lights buzz, brighter and then dimmer. "Look at you, little rabbit. No longer on the run." He shakes his head from side to side in jerky, violent motions that I fear will snap Ezra's neck. "But don't you know? Running is the only way that prey survives."

I remember seeing my mother bleeding on the floor. Hearing an axe burying itself in my father's skull. A dozen times hiding under my bed with my hands clasped over my mouth and tears streaming down my face. *Don't look at him, don't even think about him.* I'm breaking all of the rules that kept me safe for so long. But I'd rather die fighting than live in fear for a day longer.

And I am not alone. Dorian's presence reminds me of that. He steps up beside me, one hand resting on my lower back. We face Godric together, neither of us hiding. We're strongest together. Always have been.

Godric laughs, the shoulders of Ezra's body twitching like an unhinged marionette. He points one finger at me.

I try to speak but choke on nothing. Try to lift a foot, but it refuses to obey. I'm frozen in place, able only to move my eyes, which flick frantically.

Ezra lifts two fingers and slowly aims them toward Dorian. "Bang," he says.

Blood erupts from Dorian's chest.

He presses a gloved hand to the wound, and his fingers come away coated in red—but before I can scream, the blood turns to roses, a bouquet held out in his hand. He tosses the handful of flowers at Ezra, and it bursts into flame.

Ezra stumbles back, coughing, and I lurch forward, released from stasis. I rush through the smoke, but a flick of Ezra's wrist sends me hurtling down the hallway. Another, and Dorian lifts off the floor and slams into the ceiling.

But the moment he touches it, bony appendages burst from his back, and suddenly he's a spider crawling across the ceiling upside down. He drops on top of Ezra, knocking him to the floor.

Ezra raises a hand, and Dorian flies back again. But he lands on his feet, shoes skidding across the tile before he comes to a stop, none the worse for wear. Ezra snarls a curse and slices a hand through the air, and Dorian's mask cracks in half.

Dorian reaches up to cover his face with two gloved hands. But just as Ezra grins in triumph and steps forward, Dorian drops his hand and looks up again; the cracked porcelain drops to the floor and shatters, revealing another, identical mask waiting beneath. He launches himself at Ezra again, a dozen hands bursting out of his sides and reaching to grab at him.

Dorian is ever in motion, ever-changing, limited only by our combined imaginations. He is the most beautiful chaos. It feels like I'm finally getting a glimpse of what he should've always been, unrestricted by his cell or my childhood home or my own failure of imagination. He's finally free.

And his chaos is also the perfect distraction. I creep closer along the edge of the hallway, unnoticed as Ezra remains occupied by Dorian's constant, shifting blitz of attacks. He doesn't seem to notice that Dorian isn't really trying to hurt him, knowing it would hurt Ezra too. Nor does he notice me approaching until I'm just a yard away. When Dorian falls back, Ezra finally whirls to face me, one hand raised.

The tension on his face melts to annoyance when he sees me.

"Ah," he says, dripping condescension. "You."

"Yes. Me."

I grab his face with both hands. I feel that same spark I always do whenever I touch Ezra. The two of us are connected, and he is still in there, fighting.

I shut my eyes and reach into his mind. I picture a hand reaching out, and I *feel* Ezra's fingers close around mine. But instead of pulling him out of the darkness, I step into it with him.

The last thing I hear is Dorian shouting my name before the world falls away.

Chapter Twenty-Nine

"Daisy," Ezra gasps.

I lift my head as the world slowly comes into focus. I find myself in an all too familiar room. White walls, white tile, a metal table with a radio sitting on top of it…this is Dorian's cell. But it's Ezra strapped to the bed in a straitjacket.

I rush over to release him, undoing the straps on his back and pulling it off. "This isn't real," I tell him. "It's all in your mind." I remember how it felt to be trapped in a mental cage while Godric used my body.

But I broke out. Once I've released Ezra, I march over to the door to demonstrate. I raise a hand and reach for my power to crush it like I crushed it in real life—but nothing happens.

I blink, lower my hand, doubt seeping in. "*Your* mind," I repeat, turning to face Ezra. He's still sitting on the edge of the bed, his face pale and stricken. "You have to be the one to let us out of here."

"I'm not strong enough to stop him," Ezra says. "He-he killed those people. I saw it, and I couldn't do anything… I *can't* do anything."

"Don't say that." I cross the room to him and bend down to take his trembling hands in mine. Electricity sparks between us. "Do you feel that?" I ask, squeezing his fingers. "We amplify each other. We always have. And I'm here to help you now."

But he shakes his head, pulling his fingers free. "You shouldn't have come," he says. "Just do what you did before. Trap him in here with me."

"I'm not going to do that to you," I say. "There has to be another way."

"There isn't," Ezra says. "It's for the best. Trap him in my head and put me in a cell at the MRF where I can't get free."

"What?" I whisper. "Ezra…"

The radio on the table crackles to life. I turn to it, hoping Dorian has found his way to us—but instead the disturbingly cheery tune of "Run, Rabbit, Run!" begins to play.

The shutters on the viewing panel slide open, and Godric peers through from the observation room, grinning and horrible.

"One cage for two psychics," he says through the intercom, voice crackling from a speaker on the wall. "How practical."

I glower at him. "You're trapped in here too."

He shrugs. "I already did what I came here to do. Now I get to have some fun." He bends down and flips a switch on the control panel in front of him. The cell shudders around us, and then the walls start to shrink inward.

I swallow my panic. "Ezra." I squeeze his hands again. "You need to get us out of here."

"If we get out, so does he," Ezra says. "It's not safe."

"And Ezra has always known this is exactly where he belongs," Godric says, his voice full of false cheer. "He never would have worked at the MRF if he wasn't ready to end up a prisoner there. He knew he deserved it. Isn't that right, Ezra?"

"That's not true!" I say. It frightens me to see that Ezra still isn't arguing; his hand is limp in mine, and his eyes are dull, missing some vital spark. I grab him by the shoulder and shake him. "You don't deserve this. Neither of us do. We can fight him!"

The metal table creaks and bends as one of the walls reaches it. They're still closing in.

"He hoped he would get caught," Godric says. There's a screech of metal as the table gives way, and I climb onto the bed, pulling Ezra with me, because there's no space left on the floor. The room is shrinking, walls threatening to crush us. "Especially after the terrible things he did. You don't even know the half of it, Daisy! The things he's seen in this place, the experiments he's been complicit in… He's worse than a monster. A coward, a freak, a traitor—"

"You told me that yourself," Ezra whispers.

My chest aches. "I didn't. That was *him* in my body. I would never say that, because you're not any of those things." I'm done talking to Godric; I whisper directly to Ezra as the room shrinks around us.

There's not even enough space to stand on the bed. A wall presses against my back. The one behind Ezra is doing the same to him.

"You saved Dorian." I think of that day he wrote *I am like you* and changed the world for me. I smile, tears blurring my vision. "You saved *me*." I throw my arms around his neck and squeeze him. "Before you, my only friend was the one I created for myself," I tell him, holding him close. If we don't make it out of here, I at least want him to understand. "I'm so grateful for you, Ezra. I'm so grateful that we met. You made me realize I'm not alone."

The walls are on all sides now. They're pressing in, crushing the air from my lungs as I'm shoved into Ezra's chest. There's a terrible weight, a bone-cracking pressure, and then—

* * *

I shudder awake on the floor of the MRF. Dorian is cradling me in his arms.

"Ezra," I croak, and turn to see his limp body lying on the tile with blood streaming from his nose. He is completely still.

My heart lurches—but a moment later, his chest rises. Falls. Rises again. His eyes snap open and he sits up, a shaky hand pushing his glasses up his nose.

"I pushed him out," he croaks. "Don't let him get away."

I scramble to my feet alongside Dorian, but there's no sign of Godric anywhere. "He's here? I can't— I don't—"

Ezra raises a hand and points. "Right there!"

I whirl around, but there's nothing but an empty hallway. Dorian turns in a circle, eyes darting everywhere, but he seems similarly at a loss. But Ezra— Ezra is staring like he can see Godric clear as day.

I reach over, grab his hand. And suddenly I can see him too.

The demon looks a whole lot smaller outside of our heads. He's a hunched red form, wizened and withered. Pathetic and barely a few feet tall. His black eyes widen as he sees Ezra and I staring at him. He turns to run, but I thrust out a hand.

"*Stop,*" I command, and he does. One leg lifted, one hand outstretched, he freezes in place, trembling with fury and fear. "Dorian," I say, strained with the effort of holding Godric in place—but Dorian doesn't need more encouragement than that.

He falls upon his father, his killer, the demon. All four hands grasp at him. Without a vessel or time to feed, Godric suddenly seems so small and weak. And Dorian is no longer the terrified boy he once dragged out from under the bed to kill.

"You're too late," Godric snarls. "I've already released him—"

Dorian rips him limb from limb. The demon erupts in a shriek and a spray of gore, and as Dorian lets the pieces fall to the floor, they crumble away into ash and leave nothing but dust.

Chapter Thirty

Walking Dorian back to his cell is the hardest thing I've ever had to do. I cling to his hand as he steps over the threshold. He turns to face me and bends to press a chaste kiss to the back of my hand before he disappears.

"Stay right here. I'll be back," I promise the seemingly empty room. Then I walk away, fighting tears.

It would've been easy for us to escape in the chaos that happened after the fight. But Ezra and I sat side by side in the hallway, Dorian standing protectively over both of us, until the MRF's emergency services team swarmed in. Still, none of them could actually see that Dorian was free, and they're too busy tending their wounded and cleaning up bodies to chase after us until we're long gone.

But Ezra once told me to have faith, and that this was about more than me and Dorian, and I'm choosing to trust him. I owe him for all that he's done. Dorian and I *both* do.

But as I turn to head to Dr. Wright's office where we're supposed to meet her to discuss all of this, I pause. The door next to Dorian's—cell X-16—is left wide open. Fear slithers down my spine as I remember Godric's last words. *You're too late. I've already released...*

That demon came to the MRF with a plan. What kind of monster was it hoping to set free? I imagine some huge creature with horns and bloodred claws, a monstrous aberration unleashed to wreak havoc on Ash Valley. Maybe our troubles have only just begun.

I'm about to hurry past and warn Dr. Wright and the rest that a subject is free, but movement within the cell gives me pause. I stop in the doorway and look in and see a man sitting on the edge of the bed. A tall, slender young man with hair like ink and skin like porcelain. He's bent over, clutching his head.

I hesitate, confused. Is that Subject X-16? Why did Godric go through so much trouble to release what appears to be a normal young man, and why is he still in his cell when the door is wide open?

I step toward him. "Hello? Are you all right?"

He flinches at the sound of my voice, angling his shoulders away. "Don't come any closer!"

His voice slams into me like a physical force. I gasp, mind going blank, and the next thing I know I'm on my knees, my hands braced on the floor. An immense pressure weighs on my shoulder, forcing my spine to bend.

"I'm sorry," he says, and the pressure is gone as quickly as it arrived. I scramble to my feet again, heart racing. "I'm sorry! I just…something is happening. I…" He cuts off in a groan of pain, clawing at his own face. Blood drips from between his fingers.

"Let me help you," I say. Fear is weakening my knees, making it hard to breathe, but still, it's obvious he's in pain. "Tell me what I can do—"

He lowers his hand, turning to me. His eyes meet mine, and they are bloodred, burning. Pure hellfire. And in the center of his forehead, a third eye is emerging from his skin, its slit pupil focusing on me.

"Get out and shut the door," he rasps, and his voice echoes in my mind.

My mind goes white again. The next thing I am aware of, I'm standing in the hallway, in front of a closed metal door.

* * *

I rush through the door of Dr. Wright's office, breathing hard.

She turns her chair to face me with a thin smile. "There you are. I was half afraid you'd leave and—"

"There's something wrong with X-16," I blurt out.

She pauses, eyes widening in immediate concern. "*Sixteen?*"

I nod, wrapping trembling arms around myself. I explain what I saw from the moment I found his cell open, and Dr. Wright's shoulders slump in relief as I relay that I shut the door as I left.

"Well, thank God he's still contained," she murmurs.

"He seemed like he was in pain," I say. "He didn't try to hurt me or anything…"

"He never *tries* to hurt anybody," she says. "But trust me, it's good you got out of there when you did." She turns, and I realize that we're not alone in the room. On the other side of her office, a redheaded woman is seated in front of Ezra, shining a flashlight in his eyes. "Ms. Sullivan," says Dr. Wright, "I'll have to sedate him first, but would you mind taking a look at X-16 for me before you leave?"

The woman shuts off the flashlight and looks over at us, eyeing me curiously before nodding to Dr. Wright. "Whatever you need. I'm in town all weekend."

"And we are fortunate that's the case. How's our Mr. Bradford?"

Ezra looks over and flashes us a thumbs-up. "I'm good," he says, though his bruised and battered face looks far from it.

"He's mildly concussed and lucky not to have a broken nose," the redhead says dourly. "But from what I've heard, it could've been a lot worse."

"See? Even Lucy says I'm good," Ezra says. He shoots us a crooked smile and then winces from the effort.

"Not what I said." She nudges his shoulder and then stands and walks over to me. "Your face," she murmurs, studying it.

I almost forgot about the gouges Godric left across my skin when I fought him in my mind. I reach up a hand to touch the marks and wince.

"Could I take a look, and examine you for any side effects?" Lucy asks.

I shrink back from her, my mind flashing to tests and doctors and a padded cell, but at Ezra's encouraging nod, I force myself to relax. "Yes."

As she pulls up a chair beside me and begins looking over my wounds, Dr. Wright sits back in her chair and folds her arms over her chest.

"Now, while we're here… Is one of you going to tell me the truth, or is this going to be another incident that I have to write off as a freak accident?"

"I can explain," Ezra says.

"We *both* can," I say.

We share a long, loaded look. Both of us know how dangerous

the truth can be, and neither of us can give the full story unless we're both willing to lay everything out on the table. Our secrecy and lies over the last few months. Our abilities, which set us apart from normal people.

After searching my expression, Ezra nods. I turn to Dr. Wright.

"I suppose I should start by reintroducing myself," I say. "My real name is Daisy Dumont…"

* * *

It takes a long while to sort through everything that's happened over the last few months. By the time I'm done, Lucy has tended to my face, declared me otherwise healthy, and left to check on Subject X-16. Ezra has pulled his seat beside mine, and we sit with our hands clasped between us as we wait for Dr. Wright to speak.

"Well, I'm not happy with how you've handled all of this," she says, with a pointed look at Ezra. "But I suppose I can't blame you, either. I was here while the old guard was in charge of the MRF too, Ezra. I understand how afraid you must have been. But I want you to come to me with these concerns from now on."

"To you," Ezra says. "As in, not Director Ramsey?"

Dr. Wright's lips firm as though she's trying to hide a smile— but then she gives in, and they curve upward. "We haven't officially made the announcement yet, but he'll be stepping down from that position soon."

Ezra's smile is genuine. "Are congratulations in order?"

"Yes, well. I think we're all aware that I've been the one

keeping things running for a while now. Might as well make it official." She opens her desk and flicks through a stack of papers until she finds what she wants.

I clear my throat delicately. "Sorry to interrupt, and I appreciate your understanding, but…" I clench my hands in my lap, trying to stop them from trembling. "What will this mean for Dorian?"

"As Daisy just explained, Dorian is innocent," Ezra says. "He's harmless. More than that, he helped us. He saved my life, and likely the lives of countless others, by preventing Godric from walking free."

Dr. Wright looks at him—her gaze curious, assessing. "What would you have me do, Ezra?"

Ezra's grip on my hand tightens. I squeeze him back.

"I think now is the time that we decide what kind of facility we want this place to be," he says. "And if we want to be better than our predecessors, then…" He sits straighter. "We should do the right thing by setting him free. He never deserved to be locked up in the first place."

Dr. Wright twirls a pen in one hand, her expression impossible to read. "This has always been a place that captures monsters," she says. "There is a lot that you don't know, Ezra. If word of this reached the shareholders…"

"There's a lot that the shareholders don't know, too," Ezra says.

I stay quiet as they share a look. There is so much to this I don't understand, and I don't need to. I know that Dorian and I are a small part of a larger story, but all I want is for our chapter to have a happy ending.

"This is all very unorthodox," Dr. Wright says.

"When has the MRF ever been anything else?" Ezra asks,

smiling. "*You* get to decide what our new normal is, *Director* Wright."

She mirrors his smile. "You're correct," she says. "And in most cases, I would want more time to review this. But I think the facts are clear here, and given the assistance that you and X-15 have given us in our time of need, I'm willing to waive some of the formalities." She scribbles a signature on the bottom of the paper she grabbed, and pushes it across the table to me. "I'm happy to declare X-15 as our facility's first 'safe to release' subject."

It takes a moment for the words to sink in. I just sit and stare at her, my lips slightly parted. "Just like that?" I whisper, hardly able to believe it.

"It appears to me that X-15 never harmed anyone, including during this incident when he was set free. He should never have been taken into MRF custody in the first place, and I believe that he has suffered unfairly for long enough. We'll be checking in with you as things settle down here, but he can leave immediately."

Immediately. It is so much sooner than I could've hoped, and I blink away a sudden blur of tears. "Thank you," I whisper.

"You and your friend saved a lot of lives today." She reaches over to shake my hand briskly. "I should go check on Sixteen, so Ezra, if you'd like to do the honors, you should still have access to X-15's cell."

Ezra blinks, looking as stunned as I feel. "Yes, ma'am. Consider it handled."

And just like that, she leaves us.

I turn to Ezra, still fighting disbelief. He looks back at me with a tentative smile, and then we both stand and hug one another.

"You really did it," I say. "You got him released."

"You saved my life. I think we're more than even."

Ezra might not be quite as emotional about this as I am, but I know he invested a lot of energy and heart into Dorian's release as well. And after years of struggling to do some good in this horrible place, it seems he's finally made some real change.

"Thank you for trusting me," he says.

"Thank you for deserving it," I say.

"Now, let's go get Dorian out of that cell."

I nod. "Do you think…would you like to meet him, before we go? Officially, I mean?"

Ezra blinks, surprised, like he hadn't considered that. After his experiences with Godric, I wonder if maybe he's had enough monsters for a while. But to my surprise, he smiles. "I think I'd like that very much."

* * *

"Huh," Ezra says, looking at the door to cell 15. Or, rather, the empty space where the door once was; it's sitting on the floor in a twisted heap of metal. "I don't think you mentioned this part to Director Wright."

I wince. "Kind of forgot that detail."

He chuckles. We both look inside to find Dorian sitting on the bed with his hands folded in his lap, waiting patiently.

I smile, holding out a hand. "Come here."

A blink, and he's there, gloved hand enveloping mine. I step back, leading him out of the room.

"I'll just have to deactivate the barrier and grab his…" Ezra trails off, watching me. He blinks as I step back from the threshold, my hand still holding Dorian's. He may not be able to see Dorian clearly, but we're not exactly being subtle. "Ah. I see that wasn't the only detail you left out."

I shrug, unapologetic. For Ezra's sake, I wanted to give the MRF a chance to free Dorian the right way and pave a new path for the facility and its monsters. But I was never going to be leaving this building without Dorian at my side.

"Dorian," I say, squeezing his hand and looking up at him. "I'd like you to officially meet my friend Ezra."

Dorian gives me a skeptical look from behind his mask. I shoot him an exasperated one. He sighs.

Ezra lets out a small, startled noise, eyes going wide as Dorian flickers into visibility beside me.

After a long moment, Dorian extends one gloved hand. "How do you do?"

"Er…nice to meet you face to…face?" Ezra sucks in a breath and reaches out to grasp it in his. The handshake is polite, perfunctory—but then Dorian reaches out to clasp Ezra's hand with another, and then the other two, till he's holding him with all four. While Ezra stands there, baffled, Dorian inclines his long body in a bow.

"I am very grateful for your assistance in my release," he says. "And for your looking after Daisy while I was unable to. I'm glad she has a…" His eyes narrow slightly as he forces the word out. "Friend."

"Oh. Er…My pleasure. Thank you for your cooperation."

Grinning, I step forward and throw an arm around each of them, pulling them into a hug.

"Thank you both," I whisper. Then I take Dorian's hand in mine and smile up at him. "Let's go home."

Chapter Thirty-One

I wake to a sudden draft. My eyes open in the darkness as the blanket slides down over my body. It reveals my scanty nightgown, my bare legs, until I am left entirely exposed and covered in goose bumps. The blanket slides off the end of the bed. By the time it's pooled on the floor, I'm fully awake. I prop myself up on my elbows and blink sleepily at my empty bedroom.

The mattress dips beneath an invisible weight, and I feel, but don't see, fingers ghosting up over my calves, my knees, my thighs. I try to sit up, but two hands grab my wrists and pin me down. Two others slide my panties down my thighs. I gasp and squirm as he pushes my legs apart and my nightgown rucks up around my waist, leaving me bare and exposed in the cool air. Then an invisible tongue licks a hot stripe over my core.

I whimper and arch my back, wrists struggling in vain against the invisible grip. To anyone else's eyes, I would be completely alone in my room, writhing beneath nothing on the bed. I probably look insane. But I'm beyond caring about things like that at this point, especially when Dorian's ministrations are driving me toward an inevitable peak. He licks me slowly, savoring me, teasing me. The entire time, all four hands are exploring my body—cupping my breasts, clutching my hips, pressing down on my stomach to hold me in place. Only when I'm a whimpering mess does he close his invisible mouth over me and give me the steady pressure I need. I cry out loud enough to echo in the house's empty halls, and then sag back against the bed, panting.

His weight shifts, legs straddling mine, invisible torso resting against me. I wrap my arms around him and nuzzle into his neck. "Let me see you," I whisper.

He appears, his masked face inches from mine, all of him visible and beautiful...but tragically *clothed*. I frown, reaching up to run my fingers over the edges of the porcelain covering his face.

"All of you," I say. "I want to see all of you."

He pauses. I rest my fingers on the edges of his mask, but I don't try to remove it. It's his choice. I haven't seen him fully since before we were separated. Over the last couple of weeks we've been slowly getting to know each other again—figuring out how our pieces fit together—but we have yet to take this step.

He sits up, straddling my hips. First he undoes his shirt, revealing a lean chest and a flat torso with lines of muscle. He shrugs the fabric off and tosses it aside. He slides his belt off one-handed, and the pants come next, leaving him bare except for the mask and gloves. I bite my lip, looking him over from top to bottom with naked desire, my gaze lingering on the two stiff lengths just waiting for me. He's gorgeous like this, and I'll gladly take him any way I can, but I meant what I said. I want all of him. Even the parts that are less than human, even the things that would frighten anyone else. *Especially* those things, because they are the parts that are only for me.

Dorian removes his four gloves, one by one. Then he reaches up, grabs his mask, and slides it off.

My best friend, my lover, my Dorian—he does not have a face that most would consider beautiful, I suppose. But to me, he is everything I could imagine and more.

"You're perfect," I whisper. I lean up to kiss him, again and again and again. I kiss him until he is groaning, hips shifting in silent need, lips chasing mine when I pull away.

Only then do I realize we are both floating above the bed, suspended in the air. My hair floats around my head, my nightgown rippling in invisible wind.

"My perfect girl," Dorian murmurs, kissing the scars his father left across my face. "How lucky I am that you're mine."

"All yours," I whisper.

He grins. "Indeed."

Then he reaches down and rips my nightgown right off me. I gasp, and he pins my wrists above my head with one hand. Two others slide down to cup my breasts. I arch up—and then cry out at the sudden sensation of *teeth* grazing my nipples. He pulls one hand back to show me that he's grown a mouth on his palm before returning it to my breast. Before I can get used to the sensation, he's sliding against the wet heat between my thighs, and then into me, inch by slow inch. By the time he's fully sheathed, I am whimpering and thrashing beneath him. All of the furniture in the room is trembling; the lamp is floating.

"Mine," Dorian whispers, and then claims my mouth with his as he starts to fuck me. He's still teasing at my nipples with two hands, pinning my wrists with another. He spits on the fingers of his last hand and then slides it down to my ass, pushing into the tight rim. I arch against him with a mewling cry, and more hands burst out of his sides to stroke me, lick me, hold me against him. Fingers hook in my mouth, tangle in my hair; mouths nip at my jaw, suck the sensitive skin of my neck, tease my clit.

I can't possibly take more. Then his finger slides out of my ass, only for him to lift me up and guide his second cock to that tight hole.

I gasp, writhing. "I can't—"

"Of course you can," he breathes. "I'm yours. So take me. All of me."

"Yes," I whimper. He pushes into me, slowly stretching me. The pressure is overwhelming—but so is the pleasure that comes crashing in on its heels. "Yes," I say again, grinding down on his length even as tears spring to my eyes. "More, more…"

He is claiming every inch of my body. The sensations are wild. Overwhelming. Exactly what I need. I am full in a way I didn't think was possible.

"Mine," Dorian whispers in between kisses, his voice crackling with static in his desperate need. He fills me until I can't possibly take more and begins to fuck me slowly with both of his cocks, rendering me incoherent with pleasure. "All of you, all of you, *mine*. My Daisy."

He spins me and pushes me against the wardrobe, yanking my head back and making me look into the mirror so I can see the way he's ravaging me. He has no reflection, so it is only me—panting, desperate, ruined. *Perfect.*

I come with a cry that makes the entire house shake on its foundations.

* * *

To anyone else's eye, I spend a lot of time alone. A normal person wouldn't be able to hear the second set of footsteps following mine as I twirl through the halls of my house, or see the gloved hands that tweak the end of my ponytail as I run a brush through it at my vanity. But I no longer care about being normal. I've grown to quite enjoy being strange.

And my house is far from lonely.

I always have Dorian. He is there when I make tea in the morning, his long arms holding me close from behind. He is there when I climb into bed at night, his large body curled protectively around mine.

And without Godric's oppressive presence, I've begun to sense what I believe to be other spirits within the house, stirring from long slumbers. None of them have shown themselves to me yet, but I have my hopes. When they are ready to talk, I'll be here, with Dorian to help me; and if they decide that they're ready to be laid to rest, I know I can rely on Ezra's guidance and aid.

Dorian's mother won't be among them, sadly. We dug up her bones from the backyard, and handed them to the local police—along with Dorian's skeleton, relinquished to us from the MRF. The bones no longer bind Dorian, as they did to this house and then the MRF, but he was pleased that they'd be reunited with his mother's remains. Their disappearances will finally be solved after all these years, and they'll be buried together. Wherever Godric is now, I hope he's atoning for his sins, both before and after his death.

When spring comes, I plant a garden where the bodies were once buried. Dorian is learning to cook and loves to use the fresh herbs I grow.

While once I would've been content to be alone in this house with Dorian forever, now I feel enormously lucky to have Ezra as a friend as well. I enjoy my late-night diner trips with him, where he talks to me about his subjects and gives me advice on speaking to the ghosts in my home. Sometimes Dorian accompanies us; sometimes he stays in the house, or wanders Ash Valley when he's feeling particularly brave. He is free to choose where he goes now, but he almost always chooses to stay at my side.

With him, I am home, and I will never be alone again.

Acknowledgments

Thank you, dear reader, for picking up book three in my weird little monster romance series. I have so much love and appreciation for everyone who reads, rates, and reviews my work. None of this would be possible without you.

And as always, endless gratitude to the team who helped me along this journey:

My cover artist Impyeu, who never ceases to amaze me with each piece of artwork. (Check her out on Instagram, @1mpyeu!)

My brilliant developmental editor Sarah Chorn.

My sharp-sighted copyeditor Claudette Cruz ("The Editing Sweetheart").

My beta readers: Baine Fox, L&N, Katie, Alexandra, and Julie, who cheered me on and caught all manner of embarrassing early mistakes.

My ARC team, who never fail to amaze me with their enthusiasm and support.

The Romance Author's Writing Group and Indie Authors Ascending on Discord, such amazing communities who I love to learn from and laugh with.

My family, partner, and friends, who make my life worth living.

About the Author

Skyla Gray is a romance author fond of all things scary and steamy. When not writing, she can usually be found gaming, cooking, or binge-watching horror movies. She lives in Arizona with her partner and an absolute rascal of a dog.

Sign up for my newsletter for extra spicy bonus content!

You can connect with me on:

🌐 http://skyla-gray.com

🔗 https://www.instagram.com/skyla.gray.romance

Subscribe to my newsletter:

✉ https://skyla-gray.ck.page/e838b44108

Also by Skyla Gray

An Acquired Taste
Amelia is used to being referred to as an "acquired taste," but never as literally as when she becomes a professional valentine: a vampire's companion.

Overnight, Amelia goes from working late nights at a greasy LA diner to a neo-Regency world of beautiful ball gowns, glittering galas, and blood tasting notes. But her debut into vampire society only stokes her worst fears. Everyone wants to sample the unique flavor of her blood, yet nobody wants her as a long-term companion.

Nobody, that is, except for the mysterious Sebastian de Celeste. She's shocked when the handsome, notoriously reclusive vampire lord chooses her as his valentine. Yet he whisks her away to his gothic mountain estate only to avoid her company as much as possible.

Still, Amelia soon finds herself growing fond of the cranky vampire. But Sebastian has secrets, and skeletons in his closet (or rather, buried on the grounds). Amelia has had bad luck in love before, but the world of vampires is far more dangerous than the life she's used to. This time, if she trusts the wrong person, the consequences could be deadly…